A NIGHT STALKERS' STORY:

Daniel's Christmas

by
M. L. Buchman

Buchman Bookworks

Discover more by this author at: www.buchmanbookworks.com

Cover images:
Fashion portrait of lovers © Arturkurjan | Dreamstime.com
Helicopter over Baghdad © U.S. Army | Flickr
U.S. Capitol Building © Citypeek | Wikimedia
Red and green candy cane over white
© Lucie Lang | Dreamstime.com

Other works by this author:

The Night Stalkers
The Night Is Mine
I Own the Dawn
Daniel's Christmas
Wait Until Dark
Frank's Independence Day
Peter's Christmas
Wait Until Dark
Take Over at Midnight
Light Up the Night

Firehawks
Pure Heat
Wilfire at Dawn
Full Blaze

Angelo's Hearth
Where Dreams Are Born
Where Dreams Reside
Maria's Christmas Table
Where Dreams Unfold
Where Dreams Are Written

Dead Chef (thriller)
Swap Out!
One Chef!
Two Chef!

SF/F
Nara
Monk's Maze

Dieties Anonymous
Cookbook from Hell: Reheated
Saviors 101: First Book of the Reluctant Messiah

Dedication

To my lady who taught me that
there is no place like Christmas
especially when spent with those you love.

Chapter 1

Daniel Drake Darlington III pushed back further into the armchair and hung on for dear life. Without warning the seat did its best to eject him forcibly onto the floor. Only the heavy seatbelt, that was threatening to cut him in half he'd pulled it so tight, kept him in place.

"You never were the best flier."

Daniel glared at President Peter Matthews as Marine One jolted sharply left. They occupied the two facing armchairs in the narrow cargo bay of the VH-1N White Hawk helicopter. The small, three-person couch along the side was empty. The two Marine Corps crew chiefs and the two pilots sat in their seats at the front of the craft.

"I'm fine," Daniel managed through gritted teeth. "I just don't like helicopters."

President Peter Matthews sat back casually. Apparently all the turbulence that the early winter storm could hand out had not interfered with his boss' enjoyment of Daniel's discomfiture.

"And why would that be?"

The President knew damn well why his Chief of Staff hated these god-forsaken machines. Even if Marine One was probably the single safest and best maintained helicopter on the planet, he hated it from the depths of his soul along with all of its brethren of the rotorcraft category.

"My very first flight. I suffered—" a jaw rattling shake, "a bad concussion. Then we crashed."

"Yes," the President stared contemplatively at the ceiling less than foot over their heads.

Daniel kept his head ducked down so that he didn't bang it there as they flew through the next pocket of winter turbulence.

"That was one of Emily's finer flights."

And it had been. If the helicopter had been flown by anyone of lesser skill than Major Emily Beale of the Special Operations Aviation Regiment, Daniel knew he'd have been dead rather than merely bruised and battered. Thankfully the Army trained the pilots of the 160th SOAR exceptionally well, even better than the four Marines flying the President's personal craft. And Major Beale was the best among them, except for perhaps her husband.

The tape of that flight and the much more fateful flight a bare two weeks later had become mandatory training in the Army's Special Forces helicopter regiment. To this day he knew his life would have ended if he'd been aboard for that second fiery crash. The crash that had taken the First Lady's life a year ago.

But that didn't make him like this machine one whit better.

"There's home." President Matthews nodded out the window just like any tourist. Any tourist who was allowed to fly over the intensely restricted airspace surrounding the White House.

Daniel managed to look toward the window as the helicopter banked sharply to the left. Please, just let them land safely and get out of this storm. The White House did look terribly cheery. November 30th, she wasn't sporting her Christmas décor yet, but she was a majestic building, brilliantly lit, perched in the middle of the most heavily guarded park on the planet. Another jolt and he squeezed his eyes shut.

He did manage to force his eyes open as they settled flawlessly onto the lawn with barely the slightest rocking on the shock absorbers.

In moments the door slid open and a pair of Marines stood at sharp attention in their dress uniforms as if the last day of November were a sunny summer day, and not blowing freezing rain at eleven o'clock at night.

Daniel stumbled out and managed to resist the urge to kneel and kiss the ground. For one thing, it would stain the knees of his suit. For another, the President would laugh at him. Okay, he'd laugh even more than he already was.

Both feet on the ground, Daniel found himself. Managed to pull on his Chief-of-Staff cloak so to speak. He grabbed his briefcase and kept his place beside the President as they headed toward the South Entrance. They each carried umbrellas of only marginal usefulness that the Marines had thoughtfully provided. Now that they were on the ground, Daniel didn't mind the cold rain in his face. It meant he was alive.

"I'd suggest turning in right away, sir. We have an early start tomorrow."

The President clapped him on the shoulder, "Yes, Mom."

"Your mother is over in Georgetown."

"Well, I'm not going to call you 'dear' so don't get your hopes up there."

Daniel had come to really like the President. Even at the end of a brutally long day, including a flight to Kansas City, then Chicago, and back, he remained upbeat with that indefatigable energy of his. He was easy to like. There'd now be no oil workers' strike in Kansas City and his Chicago dinner speech had benefited the new governor immensely.

"You go to bed too, Daniel."

"Just going to drop off this paperwork," he held up his briefcase.

The President headed for the Grand Staircase and Daniel turned down the white marble hall and headed over to the West Wing.

Somewhere behind them in the dark, the helicopter roared back to life and lifted into the night.

Chapter 2

The phone hammered him awake. Daniel came to in his office chair with the phone already to his ear.

Someone was speaking rapidly. He caught perhaps one word in three. "CIA. Immediate briefing. North Korea."

He must have made some intelligible reply as moments later he was listening to a dial tone.

Daniel rubbed at his eyes, but the vista didn't change. Large cherry wood desk. Mounds of work in neatly stacked folders that he'd sat down to tackle after the long flight. His briefcase still unopened on the floor beside him. Definitely the Chief of Staff's office. His office. Nightmare or reality? Both. Definitely.

Phone. He'd been on the phone.

The words came back and, now fully awake, Daniel started swearing even as he grabbed the handset and began dialing.

Maybe he could blame all this on Emily Beale. In the three short weeks she'd been at the White House, Daniel had risen from being the First Lady's secretary to the White House Chief of Staff and it was partly Emily's fault. As if his life had been battered by a tornado. Still felt that way a year later.

Okay, call it mostly her fault.

As he listened to the phone ringing in his ear, it felt better to have someone to blame. He rubbed at his eyes. A year later and he still didn't know whether to curse Major Beale or thank her.

Maybe he could make it all her fault.

"Yagumph."

"Good morning, Mr. President."

"Is it morning?" The deep voice would have been incomprehensibly groggy without the familiarity of long practice.

Daniel checked his watch, barely morning. "Yes, sir!" he offered his most chipper voice.

"Crap! What? All of 12:03?"

"12:10, sir." They'd been on the ground just over an hour.

"Double crap!" The President was slowly gaining in clarity, maybe one in ten linguists would be able to understand him now.

"Seven more minutes of sleep than you guessed, sir."

"Daniel?"

"Yes, Mr. President?"

"Next time Major Beale comes to town, I'm sending you up on one of her training rides."

"Sounds like fun, sir." If he had a death wish. "Crashing in the Lincoln Memorial Reflecting Pool is definitely an experience I can't wait to relive." The Major was also the childhood friend of the President, so he had to walk with a little care, but not much. The two of them were that close.

"Time to get up, sir, the CIA is coming calling. They'll be here in twenty minutes."

"I'll be there in ten." A low groan sounded over the phone. "Make that fifteen." The handset rattled loudly as he missed the cradle. Daniel got the phone clear of his ear before the President's handset dropped on the floor.

Daniel hung up and considered sleeping for the another fifteen minutes. There was a nice sofa along the far wall sitting in a close group with a couple of armchairs, but he'd have to stand up to reach it. All in strong, dusky red leather, his secretary's doing after discovering Daniel had no taste. Janet had also ordered in a beautiful oriental rug and several large framed photographs. Even on the first day she'd known him well enough to chose images of wide-open spaces. He missed his family farm, but the photos helped him when D.C. was squeezing in too hard.

If he didn't stand and resisted the urge to seek more sleep, all that remained was to consider his desk. Its elegant cherry wood surface lost beneath a sea of reports and files.

Fifteen minutes. He could read the briefing paper on Chinese coal, review tomorrow's agenda which, if he were lucky, might stay on schedule for at least the first quarter hour of a planned fourteen-hour day. Or he could just order up a giant burn bag and be done with the whole mess.

He picked up whatever was on top of the nearest stack.

An Advent calendar.

Janet, had to be.

Well, the woman had taste. It was beautiful; encased in a soft, tooled-leather portfolio and tied closed with a narrow red ribbon done up in a neat bow. He pulled a loose end and opened the calendar. Inside were three spreads of stunning hand-painted pictures on deep-set pages. He took a moment to admire the first one.

It was a depiction of Santa and his reindeer. Except Santa might have been a particularly pudgy hamster and the reindeer might have been mice with improbable antlers. One might have had a red nose, or he might have had his eggnog spiked; the artist had left that open to interpretation. A couple of rabbits were helping to load the sleigh. Little numbered doors were set in the side of the sleigh, as well as in a nearby tree, and in the snow at the micedeer's paws. The page was thick enough that a small treat could be hidden behind each little door.

He shook the calendar lightly and heard things rattling. Probably little sweets and tidbits to hit his notorious sweet tooth.

The day Janet retired he'd be in so much trouble. Not only did she manage to keep his life organized, she also managed to make him smile, even when things were coming apart at the seams. Midnight calls from the CIA for immediate meetings didn't bode well, yet here he was dangerously close to enjoying the moment.

He started to open the little door with a tiny golden number "1" on the green ribbon pull tab. The door depicted a candy-cane colored present perched high on the sleigh.

"Don't do that."

He looked up.

A woman stood in the doorway, closely escorted by one of the service Marines. A short wave of russet hair curled partly over her face and trickled down just far enough to emphasize the line of her neck. Her bangs ruffled in a gentle wave covering one eye. The eye in the clear shone a striking hazel against pale skin. She wore a thick, woolen cardigan, a bit darker than her hair, open at the front over an electric blue turtleneck that appeared to say, "Joy to the World." At least based on the letters he could see.

"Don't do what?"

"Don't open it early," she nodded toward the calendar in his hands. "That's cheating."

He double-checked his watch. "It's twelve-eighteen on December first. That's not cheating."

"Not until nighttime, after sunset. That's what Mama always said."

"And your Mama is always right?"

"Damn straight." Though her expression momentarily belied her cheerful insistence.

He glanced at the Marine. "Kenneth. Does she have a purpose here?"

She sauntered into his office as if it were her own living room and an armed Marine was not following two paces behind her. More guts than most, or a complete unawareness of how close she was to being wrestled to the ground by a member of the U.S. Military.

"Remember what they say about the book and the cover?"

"Sure, don't judge." He inspected her wrinkled black corduroys and did his best not to appreciate the nice line they made of her legs.

She dropped into one of the leather chairs in front of his desk and propped a pair of alarmingly green sneakers with red laces on the cherry wood. At least they were clean. All she'd need to complete the image would be to pop a bright pink gum bubble at him. And maybe some of those foam slip-on reindeer antlers. He offered her a smile as she slouched lower in the chair. In turn, she offered him a clear view most of the way to her tonsils with a massive yawn.

She managed to cover it before it was completely done.

"Sorry, I've been up for three days researching this. Director Smith said I should bring it right over." She waved a slim portfolio at him that he hadn't previously noticed.

CIA Director Smith. Well, that explained who she was. Whatever lay in that portfolio was the reason he'd only had forty-five minutes of sleep so far tonight. And he'd spent that slumped in his chair. He did his best to surreptitiously straighten his jacket and tie.

"You've been researching." Maybe a prompt would get her to the point more quickly.

"Yes, Mr. Darlington. I'm Dr. Alice Thompson, with dual masters in Afghani and Mathematics at Columbia. Which makes me a dueling master. PhD in digital imaging at NYU and an analyst for the CIA.

Which means something, but I have no idea what. The reason you're awake right now is to meet with me."

"No, the reason I'm awake right now is to meet with both you and the President."

"The President?" She jerked upright in her chair, her feet dropping to the floor. "No one said anything about that to me." She twisted right and left as if seeking a place to hide.

"And it's Dr. Darlington of Tennessee. Degrees in agriculture at University of Kentucky—"

"Go Wildcats," she mumbled automatically without losing her somewhat frantic expression.

Daniel wondered how a New York girl living in D.C. would know that, but didn't sidetrack to ask.

"Poli Sci at Yale, and socio-economics at Princeton where I had the great opportunity to study cooperative economic game theory with Dr. Nash." And why he felt the need to brag to this lady once again settling in his office chair like she was hanging out in a college dorm room remained a bit of a mystery. He didn't feel sleepy anymore watching her across the mess that he called a desk. Instead he found himself truly smiling.

"You didn't really wake the President for this meeting, did you?" Her voice was little more than a whisper as she struggled to fight her body upright in the chair. She leaned forward far enough for the cardigan to fall open and reveal that the front of her turtleneck actually read "Oy to the World."

Daniel offered her his blandest smile and would have admired how snugly the material clung to her frame, but he couldn't look away from those hazel-green eyes.

"You did wake him?" her whisper more than a little panicked.

"I wish he hadn't." The President entered as she spoke. "Does this mean I can I go back to bed?"

#

Alice spun around to face the man who had come up beside her unnoticed. Tall, even more handsome than on TV. Stained sweat pants and a faded sweatshirt from Oxford didn't detract from the image in the least.

The President held out a hand. She offered her own in some ingrained social response mechanism, like a trained puppy, only to find her paw shaken and released before she had a chance to do more than allow her arm to be moved up and down.

He settled into the chair beside her before she belatedly remembered you were supposed to stand when the President arrived. He propped his sneakered feet on the edge of Dr. Darlington's beautiful cherry wood desk right where hers had been. What had she been thinking when she'd done that? Had she hoped to fluster the man and his immaculate three-piece suit behind the desk? Or had she felt so comfortable around him she hadn't cared? Must have been the first but it felt like the second.

Daniel leaned forward, "Don't worry. The complete intimidation wears off eventually. He's not all that important really; it only feels as if he is."

"Hey, I'm the one who they elected President. And I'm not a 'he.' I'm a POTUS to you."

"Right, and I'm just the guy who makes sure that the all-important President of the United States doesn't screw up at 12:30 in the morning."

"True, true." The President nodded sagely and the guys traded smiles. The mutual respect and friendship was clear between them.

They made an interesting contrast. The President had all of the magnetism she'd seen on TV, and more again in person. Even sleepy-eyed and wearing sweats, dark hair ranging loose down to his collar, he looked as if he should be framed up on a wall. Most popular President in recent history, probably all the way back to JFK. The world's ultimate bachelor since his wife's tragic death in the helicopter crash.

Whereas Dr. Darlington was perhaps the most beautiful man she'd ever seen. Yale and Princeton; *Bulldogs and Lions. Along with the Wildcats* that made two cats and a dog, that part of her mind that collected useless garbage offered up. The White House Chief of Staff looked like a classic surfer bum with those sparkling blue eyes and gold-blond hair, despite the short cut of it and his sharp three-piece suit that he filled really, really nicely.

She'd always been a nerd, only comfortable with other analyst nerds, but even her few moments with Daniel had been easy.

Before she could stop herself, she caught herself glancing over at his hands.

No ring.

Some insane part of her brain said, "Goody."

If she could slap it, she would.

Way too classically Alice. "Oh look, an intriguing rabbit hole, I think I'll fall down it." Of course, she usually fell for useless pretty boys. She'd bet that phrase had never been used to describe the White House Chief of Staff. Beautiful and, by reputation at least, brilliant as well. He was so far out of her league that it almost hurt. Still, she did wish she'd worn something nicer than her Christmas turtleneck and the old cardigan she'd knit a couple years back. It was her comfort sweater, made in a dozen shades of autumn forest browns and dusky reds.

"So, Dr. Alice Thompson, what did you bring us?" The Chief of Staff was back, all smooth and businesslike. He glanced up and over her head. "We're good here, Kenneth. Thanks."

She tipped her head back on the chair far enough to see the upper part of the upside-down Marine, her shadow who she'd completely forgotten about, looming close behind her. He offered a precise nod, did a neat snap turn, and walked out of her range of view with the back of his perfect white hat being the last thing to disappear.

Her head spun a little as she brought it back upright. She really needed some sleep.

Then she remembered what she held in the thin portfolio. It had kept her awake for three days, it would keep her going a bit longer.

That and the fact that, no matter how casual and collected he'd sounded, Dr. Daniel Drake Darlington III's hands still hadn't moved from the pull tab on the Advent calendar.

#

Daniel couldn't help noticing the quirk of a smile across Dr. Thompson's lips. With the unruly mop of hair, it was hard to tell, but she appeared to be staring at his hands.

He looked down.

The Advent calendar still lay in his lap. His hand half an inch from grabbing the little number "1" ribbon. Still.

Her smile bloomed, but she'd shaken down a few more of those soft-flowing curls and her eyes were almost invisible, except as a bright glint. Damn, it was about the cutest thing he'd ever seen.

He slapped the calendar closed and dropped it atop the nearest stack of papers. It over-balanced the stack, which slid to the right. In his sleep deprived state, he was nowhere near fast enough to stop the falling dominos as Chinese manufacturing cascaded into Arctic ecology and on into the Baja oil spill. Daniel rescued the calendar, but the oil spill took out the most recent fisheries and timbers trade reports. The budget was almost big enough to stop the whole thing, would have been if it weren't sitting on top of the east Africa political report he'd been trying to review for the last three days.

The budget slammed to the floor with a crash loud enough that they all jumped a bit. A minor blizzard of paper followed it to the oriental carpet.

Kenneth stuck his head back in the door, but the President waved him off. All Daniel could do was watch the out-of-control disaster as file folders spilled open one after another to release a fresh splash of white and blue sheets of paper. Spreading like some cubist piece of floor performance art.

The President glanced at the pile of reports fluttering to a landing beside his chair.

"Janet is gonna be so pissed at you," his boss practically crowed at him.

"Janet?"

Daniel heard Alice's voice, tentative for a moment.

"His secretary. She's lethal about Daniel's methods of organization."

Alice stretched up to peer at the disaster beyond the President's chair.

Then she aimed that impossibly cute smile at Daniel. This time those twin, hazel-colored laser beams were exposed with an easy head shake that flopped her hair back.

"How soon does she get in? Can we watch? Where do we get popcorn?"

Chapter 3

Daniel read through the CIA intelligence report for the third time.

"If this is right, we'll need a very unique asset."

POTUS looked over at him, "I know just who to call. Even if it's not a 'go' yet, we can start moving the asset into position."

Daniel nodded. "We can do it from the Game Room." He started around his desk, but had to double-back around the other side to avoid the paper disaster. His watch claimed barely one a.m.; there'd be plenty of time to fix it before Janet arrived and sentenced him to death by paper cuts.

He arrived by Alice's chair as she offered another jaw-cracking yawn.

"Sorry. I— Sorry."

She'd slipped even lower in the chair, far enough that the only thing keeping her from flowing down onto the floor were her knees bumping into the front panel of his desk.

He offered a hand to help her to her feet.

She did her one-eyed inspection of him for a moment, then accepted the offer. Her hand was deceptively strong for how fine-fingered and delicate it appeared. She rose to her feet in a smooth, fluid motion that bespoke some form of training. He'd seen it before somewhere.

"Ballet?" He knew it was wrong even as he said it.

"Sad."

"Why are you calling me sad?" Daniel knew he was missing something.

She laughed, a bright, merry sound that he could only describe as elfin, though she wasn't but a few inches shy of his own five-eleven.

"S. A. D."

"You're S.A.D.?" he barely managed to choke out.

Even the President looked shocked by that one.

The Special Activities Division was the CIA's black ops squadron. They were better trained than even the Army Rangers and were deployed in far more questionable situations.

She grinned wickedly, "Now you're the one saying I'm sad? I'm half tempted to say, 'yes,' just to see you twitch. But no. They offered us senior analysts a month of S.A.D. training to better appreciate what could and couldn't be done in the field. Found I liked the physical part, though I'd never be crazy enough to go for field ops. There's an on-going course at the gym. I don't do the weapons or field skills, but there's dance, yoga, strength training. I keep that up."

Daniel tried to get to the gym a little each day and do some weight training. He had the sudden feeling that, despite being a slip of a woman, she could probably beat the stuffing out of him. And senior analyst? If she was much past twenty-six or seven, he'd be shocked. Senior analysts usually sported decades of experience.

She freed her hand, which he didn't realize he'd still been holding until its soft, strong warmth had been removed. She turned to follow the President who waited by the door. Alice Thompson passed close enough for Daniel to smell the woman, past her soap or shampoo; a heady scent of springtime in winter washed over him. She left him wobbly on his feet, as if he were the one who hadn't slept in three days.

She and the President both stood at the door watching him.

"You coming?" Peter Matthews offered him a knowing smile over Dr. Thompson's shoulder.

And Dr. Alice Thompson merely offered that crazy, elfin laugh.

All Daniel knew was that he couldn't wait for next opportunity to get that close to her again.

Chapter 4

"You said we were going to the Game Room. This is—" Alice nearly choked on her words as she watched Daniel press a palm against a glass plate reader. She'd been tired enough to not think much as they descended from the main level down a long flight of stairs.

She didn't need the two Marine Guards at perfect attention to indicate what lay behind these heavy doors. She'd seen enough movies to know they stood at the entry to the Situation Room. A place that in many ways served as the political center of the planet. Decisions made here affected global politics, started and ended wars.

"Game Room. Definitely." Mr. Smooth-Chief-of-Staff Daniel Darlington was back in place. "Most administrations call it the Woodshed, but President Matthews is Washington D.C. born and bred. Didn't seem appropriate."

Alice still couldn't believe that she'd flustered the White House Chief of Staff. She. Alice. It was pretty flattering. Well, maybe it was lack of sleep that warped her perceptions, though she felt alarmingly awake at the moment, even if her body didn't.

"There are refreshments," the President spoke in such a friendly, normal fashion that it was proving difficult to remain gobsmacked by being in the President's presence. "An amazing video system attended by the finest Marine Corps technicians. Global politics is more like chess than say, Chutes and Ladders, but there are pieces always in motion and we try to keep track of them in here. So, the Game Room fits."

The Marines pulled back the double doors and Alice felt herself sucked inward as if by a vacuum.

Without preamble, President Matthews called out to what appeared to be an empty room, "I need to speak with Majors Beale and Henderson. They're probably still at that little SOAR base in Pakistan."

A disembodied voice spoke in soft, clearly articulated tones, "A few minutes, Mr. President."

"Pakistan?" she whispered to Daniel. With relations the way they were in Pakistan, it was hard to imagine that there was a U.S. airbase still there. Though with SOAR. Maybe. The Army's Special Operations Aviation Regiment often showed up in the damnedest places on her reports. The Night Stalkers, as they called themselves, were even called on by the CIA's S.A.D. because no one could deliver a crew by helicopter the way SOAR could. Or get them back out as consistently. Though CIA pilots would never agree, Alice had seen the reports and it was true.

"Pakistan," the President confirmed. "A special deal. Bati airbase is a small desert location that gives our folks close access to the Hindu Kush passes between Pakistan and Afghanistan. Their primary mission there is to curtail the massive arms flow that Pakistan is sponsoring. However, in exchange for the airbase and certain other considerations, the Pakistan government also receives, shall we say, stabilization assistance along their contested border with India."

That was just about the craziest arrangement she'd ever heard. But it also explained the oddities of the mission to take down Osama bin Laden. SOAR helicopters had penetrated deep into Pakistan as if coming out of nowhere, no reports ever emerged of where the flight had begun. One leak said northern Afghanistan, but that made even less sense. But perhaps from the secret, Pakistan-sanctioned airbase at the foot of the Hindu Kush mountains. That would explain the infiltration issues she'd been unable to puzzle out.

After they'd raided bin Laden's compound, they fled the country while being chased across the border by Pakistani jets. They must have been very slow jets to allow the helicopters fly from so far in-country, get clear of Pakistan airspace, and fly out over international waters. Or they had a secret pact with the government. Therefore, the Pakistani jets had chased the American helicopters for form's sake, but not been allowed to interfere because of special on-going military agreements. That made the whole bin-Laden operational logistics make sense, finally.

Alice appreciated that. There was a back-burner portion of her thought processes that worried and chipped away at unexplained problems. That one had been there for a year or more, and now she could tell by the sudden mental silence that enough of the pieces were in place and she could let it go.

It also illustrated different aspects of the notorious southwest Asian schizophrenia. It was the reason her job never grew dull. It was like they thought with both sides of their brain, separately. Iran, a paranoid, extreme Islamic nation that cast aside all things Western, was now one of the few space powers on the planet. Afghanistan, desperate to shed the mantel of the Taliban, reviled the U.S. presence to suppress the brutally violent fanatics. The dichotomy of thought and action remained endlessly fascinating.

Daniel offered her some coffee and a doughnut. But her nervous system was so scrambled with exhaustion that she settled for hot chocolate and a croissant to avoid the bizarre effects caffeine perpetrate.

As they sat at the table, the giant screen at the end of the room lit up. A beautiful blond glared balefully out at them.

"What the hell do you want at this hour, Sneaker Boy?"

Sneaker Boy? Alice looked around to see who she was addressing. The President was smiling at the screen.

"Morning, Squirt. What are you so surly about?" There was a tease in his voice.

Daniel leaned over to whisper in her ear, "Childhood friends."

Alice turned to glance at him which brought them nearly nose-to-nose. Just the slightest bit of lean and they'd be kissing. She looked away quickly and took a large bite of her croissant to cover just how stupid her brain could be when she was tired. Her cat would be laughing at her for being such a goofball. If she had a cat.

The woman on the screen covered her face with both her hands as if impossibly weary. "Peter, you idiot!"

Alice choked, coughed, and spewed a small cloud of flaky croissant crust all over the polished Sit Room conference table.

"What time is it?" clearly meant as a rhetorical question. Rhetorical with an acid bite.

"One a.m. our time," the President responded pleasantly. "Makes it midday for you."

The woman uncovered one eye and just scowled at the President.

"Oh, right." He didn't sound very chagrined.

Alice finally got it, too. The Night Stalkers were called that for a reason. They lived in a flipped clock world, flying missions at night, sleeping during the day. The President had just rousted them after two or maybe three hours of sleep. And by the look of it, last night had included an exhausting mission.

She idly wondered if a report of it might be crossing her desk at the CIA even now. No, she'd left the southwest Asia desk six months ago. For half a year she'd been specializing in the craziest, most isolationist country on the planet.

And when she'd pulled her latest report on North Korea together, the Director had sent her scampering to the White House to report.

The Night Stalkers. The President had asked for Majors Beale and Henderson. That meant this was Major Emily Beale. Alice inspected the sleepy woman more closely. She'd shown up in enough of Alice's reports over the years for her to know about the legend the woman had become. She out flew everyone, with the possible exception of her even more famous husband. Well, famous to the very small world of those who knew about black ops helicopter pilots.

All Alice saw was a sleepy looking woman in a sand-colored t-shirt.

"At least I didn't wake Mark."

A square chin in need of a shave appeared over Beale's shoulder, "I wish, Mr. President."

A hand reached out and filled the screen for a moment as it realigned the camera a bit higher. The two most successful pilots in SOAR history now looked out at them. Their most captivating features were Henderson's gray eyes and Beale's brilliant blues, almost as bright as Daniel's. Even rumpled, tired, and grumpy, they made a beautiful couple.

Alice had always wondered how she'd look as part of a couple. Her sporadic relationships typically burned out long before her imagination had time to really take hold. And any efforts to make a portrait-type image, even in her head, had never gelled. Even in her naïve teenage years she hadn't been able to imagine herself a couple with her massive crush, Leonardo di Caprio. And by the time *Firefly's* Nathan Fillion came along, she'd lost the dreamy-eyed teenager completely.

She glanced again at the profile of the man seated beside her in his three-piece suit in the depths of a Washington D.C. night. Daniel was concentrating on the screen at the moment, revealing only his profile.

Him she could picture easily.

Chapter 5

Alice was positively weaving by the time they left the Situation Room and passed by the Marine guards.

Daniel offered his arm.

She slipped her hand through the crook of his elbow, as if they were a couple promenading through a formal garden rather than striding along the West Wing basement hallway. Alice took a deep breath, trying not to acknowledge how much she enjoyed the feeling.

"Set her up in one of the spare rooms." The President nodded to her.

Stay in the White House? She stumbled on the carpeted steps, would have tumbled to the ground if not for Daniel's support. Yet another proof to her mother that she lacked any of the grace that ten years of childhood ballet should have taught her.

"I'll get her settled and be right back down, Mr. President."

Not that she'd stay awake long enough to get back to her apartment. Once she'd handed off the information that had kept her awake for three days, she felt limp.

"No, we're done. We needed to get Emily in motion. Next steps tomorrow. I'm just going to swing through the office for a minute and then go back to bed."

At the head of the stairs, Daniel turned her to the right, resting his left hand over her own where it curled about his right forearm. The sudden warmth felt both startling and comforting as her fingers were freezing cold by contrast. She'd pushed through enough M-LOS projects, as she called the ones causing massive lack of sleep, to know her body would go through chills and dizziness until she had at least a half dozen hours under her belt.

The chill only deepened as they walked the West Colonnade, passing the Marines standing stock still in heavy winter coats, rifles at the ready.

"They do that all winter?"

"I know. Pretty wild, hunh?" He pretended a shiver that she could feel through his arm, even as one of the Marines opened the door for them to enter the Residence.

In moments they were inside the Palm Room, Daniel acting the genial tour guide. His words blurred beneath the grandeur of everything. The room, little more than a pass-through with a bench, a marble table, and some potted palms, was alive with lacy woodwork and watched over by clearly historic paintings of Lady Liberty. The double doors beyond led to a wide, red-carpeted hallway, marble archways, chandeliers.

"Where's the Christmas decorations?" she'd never actually been to the White House before and was sad that she'd be missing them.

"Not here yet."

She bit back her disappointment. Of course, for an analyst to sit in the Situation Room and watch the first piece in the next game move across the board, that was a pretty good treat as well.

"Now you've done it, Alice."

"What was that?" Daniel turned to face her.

"Fallen down the rabbit hole."

Daniel's laugh was easy, comfortable, and helped bring the whole place back into a little perspective.

"I thought Alice had long blond curls on her trip to Wonderland." He led her into a mahogany-lined elevator.

"Mama hoped, but I ended up with this." Or maybe it was walnut.

Daniel was quiet long enough for her to look up at him as they rode smoothly upward to the number three he had punched.

He was looking down at her. She'd need serious heels to be eye-to-eye with him. She'd never been good at heels.

"No, blond isn't you. Russet suits you perfectly."

"Always thought of it more as mouse-brown."

"No. Russet. A beautiful russet red."

She glanced back up at him as he led her out of the elevator to see if he was making fun of her. He studied the top of her head with a look of intense concentration. As if he were ascertaining an initial assessment of a situation rather than the bit of a flirt she'd expected. He was the perfect straight man.

"Like a russet potato?" she was never able to resist prodding a straight man.

"No. I meant the color of roses at sunset." She tried to catch her breath, but hadn't succeeded by the time he led her to a spacious bedroom. Even if she'd wanted to continue the conversation, all her body saw was somewhere to stretch out.

"Kitchen over that way if you get hungry."

Hungry? The word didn't anchor to anything in particular. It was still consumed by bed and sleep.

"President lives on the Second Floor, so don't be concerned about disturbing him."

Some saving grace there.

"I'm the First Chief of Staff to live here in decades. It was a little strange at first, but I'm getting used to it."

"Hungry." Her lagging brain finally found a use for the word. Hungry for a beautiful man who said her hair was the color of roses at sunset.

"I'm just across the hall if you need anything."

Needed anything.

She went up on her tiptoes, rested a hand on that nice, broad chest of his to steady herself, and kissed him.

He didn't respond at first. She could feel the shock and surprise warring in him. All the propriety you'd expect from a gentleman.

Too much, Alice. Too forward. But the warmth of his lips, the strength of his muscles beneath her palm held her in place a moment longer.

A moment just long enough for Daniel to return the kiss.

A gentle, tentative gesture that in moments heated to melting. Specifically, her melting against him as his hands wrapped around and supported her. As his mouth explored hers.

Alice heard a small moan. She'd never in her twenty-seven years moaned when she kissed a man. But the sound was too high to come from Daniel, so it must have been hers.

She wallowed in being cradled in his arms, in being held as if she was someone desirable, even precious.

The change came suddenly. A freeze. A breath of space. A whispered, "sorry."

"I'm not." She opened her eyes, she didn't recall closing them, and looked up at the summer-sky blue ones inspecting her.

Okay, this was awfully forward for her. She'd be more likely to go a half-dozen dates and barely hold hands, than to kiss a stranger.

But she wasn't sorry. Especially not with a man who could kiss like that.

"You're an amazing kisser."

Daniel blinked at her. Sliding his hands down her arms until he held her hands. His were big, warm hands. Strong. Not what you'd expect from a paper-pusher.

"I'd best say goodnight."

"Sure you don't want to tuck me in?" She slapped her hand over her mouth. She'd never said such a Mae West line in her entire life. Next she'd be asking him if he knew how to whistle.

He slid a hand up to cradle her cheek.

"I'd love to, which is exactly why I'm not going to." He kissed the back of her hand where it still covered her mouth.

"Now go."

With gentle hands, he turned her to face the bedroom, and pushed lightly against her shoulders to send her forward.

A soft click indicated the door had closed behind her.

The hand that yet covered her mouth was no longer cold. Instead it was warm with the heat of the kiss she could still feel against the back of it.

Chapter 6

Daniel had spent most of his lunch hour in the workout room. Now, he was reading through the overnight reports, ones that he'd been trying to get to since breakfast, over a quick lunch of a BLT sandwich and a Coke when she came into the kitchen.

She entered the kitchen from behind him, but he didn't doubt that it was Dr. Alice Thompson for a single second. The President would have arrived with his normal bravado and be already in the middle of a sentence before the door was even open. A trait he shared with his deceased wife, a comparison Daniel kept to himself as the man would not have appreciated it. If it had been the Secret Service entering the room, as they would have done if the President was in tow, there'd be at least two sets of very business-like footsteps.

But there weren't.

The kitchen door opened part way, paused for a long moment, and then swung a bit farther. No soft slap of the rubber soles the agents wore for traction, but instead the almost silent step of a pair of sneakers on a woman who weighed half as much your average Secret Service agent.

"Good afternoon, did you sleep well?"

He didn't turn to look at her, but remained instead perched on his stool, his reports spread out across the light and dark stripes of the maple-and-cherry wood island. Didn't want to acknowledge the advantage he'd taken of an exhausted woman. He'd wanted to take that advantage though. For the first time in a long time, he really wanted to. Daniel tried not to cringe and simply hoped that she wouldn't recall how he had kissed her.

She wasn't drunk, you idiot. Just tired.

"I guess. Not really awake yet. Did you get any sleep?" She drifted into his peripheral vision over by the refrigerator.

"Not much." Not at all really. First he'd gone back down to his office to clean up the mess. Then the phone rang and he'd clarified the instructions the President had set in motion half-a-world away. That was the problem when he and the President classified something "need to know" only, all the little questions shot straight to the top.

Then he saw the report newly placed in the middle of the teetering stacks on top of his desk. The upcoming G-8 summit had just had another bomb threat which led to a meeting with the Secret Service detail in charge of arranging that. One thing led to the next as he caught up with e-mail, fired off instructions to his staff for the morning. The overnighters discovered he was awake and began routing their questions to him.

Around three-thirty a.m. the President had drifted in from the Oval Office, "just to see if Daniel was available." They'd spent the next hour reviewing and revising the new South African trade agreement, which had involved rousting the policy analysts from bed to straighten out an addition that someone had slipped in about Japanese whaling rights around Cape Horn. All of which had to be in place by five a.m. local-time before the eleven o'clock African-time round of talks restarted in Johannesburg.

When Janet arrived at six-thirty, Daniel had managed to clean up exactly three papers from the foot-deep stack that spread all the way under the couch beside his desk. With the rough edge of her contempt for how he let his desk become so out of control in first place, all communicated articulately by her not uttering a single word, she had it completely reorganized in less than twenty minutes.

Daniel hadn't even tried to go to bed, especially not just across the hall from Dr. Alice Thompson. He'd been too aware of her from all the way over in the West Wing. Here in the residence, way too close.

The only reason he'd come over now was for a workout and late lunch. The break helped recenter him before the typical afternoon mêlée.

Some part of him had thought Dr. Alice Thompson would have long since been awake and gone. And some part of him had known she still slept across the hall.

He waved a hand toward the refrigerator, "Help yourself." Then he tried to recall the notation he'd been intending to write in the report's margin which lay open before him. Completely vanished.

Tossing down the pen, he sighed in frustration. He didn't even know what the report was about at the moment. All he could think about was how much he wanted to taste her kiss again. *You aren't a sixteen-year old dying of hormones,* he instructed himself; which had no affect at all on the path of his thoughts.

"Sorry to interrupt you, maybe I should just go." She turned for the door.aniel ran a hand through his hair. "No, this is a never-ending quest here at the White House. The elusive Completed Task."

"Maybe if you hunted it with …"

"A butterfly net?"

She laughed. It was a light, merry sound. One quickly muffled by the hand she raised to cover her mouth.

In that moment Daniel discovered just how much he enjoyed making her laugh.

"Please," he waved at the refrigerator again. "I can make you coffee or tea."

A quick glance checking once more for permission, she finally opened the door and peeked inside the stainless steel monster. "Juice is fine." She took a bottle. And a container of Greek yogurt.

"Or the chefs could make you a proper lunch." He pointed toward the silverware drawer for a spoon.

"I think breakfast will be fine. And this is good, honestly."

She went to sit across the island from him and peeked into the open box in the middle of the counter. "Ooo, Christmas cookies!"

"Help yourself."

"I couldn't. They're so beautiful."

Daniel looked in. They were. "Old family tradition. We make cookie boxes for anyone, family or close friends, who can't be around for the holiday baking. My big sister probably made most of these." He poked around until he found a gingerbread man sticking out its tongue at him. He held it up for Alice to see. "Definitely Melanie."

She took a reindeer that had one leg lifted to relieve itself against an elf. "You sure I'm not interrupting?"

"No need to be so tentative. Please, join me. It has to be better than," he had to flip to the cover of the report to remember what it addressed, "Pacific Northwest Reforestation."

It wasn't that she was just hesitant. He watched as she settled onto the bar stool opposite him. He'd shared several meals here with Emily Beale when she'd been posing as the First Lady's chef. Major Beale cooked like a magician and looked like a modern-day warrior goddess. . And while it was hard not to be stunned by that, combined with her military achievements, it was also exhausting. The woman was driven in a way that left even the President breathless.

It was an interesting contrast to Dr. Alice Thompson, sitting exactly where Emily Beale had sat across from him just a year before. The steel backbone, the warrior's reflexes, and the black-and-white razor of the Captain's mind contrasting with the quiet thoughtfulness of Dr. Thompson.

Alice was, Daniel had to cast about his mind until he found it, she was shy. An odd and unusual feature in the world of political extroverts who constituted the bulk of the White House Staff. Perhaps last night had been an aberration, her relaxed attitude and quick ripostes a result of guards lowered by exhaustion.

He knew that having missed last night's sleep, he'd be in a similar state by late afternoon. But at the moment, he'd rather put her at her ease.

"About last night, I'm—"

"Not the least bit sorry." She cut him off. Her head popped up just enough from where it had been concentrating on her yogurt for him to see that one eye peeking out from under her bangs.

Well, no question remained regarding her memory.

"You're luscious."

Daniel found himself dangerously close to a blush. Clearing his throat didn't seem appropriate, something his father would do.

He had to say, something. "Uh, so are you."

That earned him the head toss that cleared both of her eyes and revealed that smile that had lit up his imagination last night.

"Good thing we'll never see each other again then, hunh?"

Daniel could feel himself blanch. Never see her again? No. That couldn't be... "You're teasing?"

"Oooo," Alice clapped her hands and rubbed them together as if preparing for evil deeds. "A gudgeon! This is going to be fun."

"A what?"

"A small fish."

Daniel did his best to glare at her, but she didn't appear daunted in the slightest.

"It's also military slang for someone who will take a straight line, hook and sinker. Straight man. Gudgeon. Dr. Drake Darlington. All one and the same."

Then she slapped a hand over her mouth again and her eyes grew quite wide and very distressed, looking as comic as she had last night right after he'd kissed her. And she'd kissed him back. Nothing wrong with his memory either.

He couldn't stop the laugh.

"Sorry," she mumbled through her fingers. "I promise I'll cut my tongue out later."

"I'll help." *Gudgeon indeed.* He could keep up just fine.

Chapter 7

"I can find the front door on my own." Alice wished she had on much more sophisticated clothes. What had been comfortable at one in the morning looked very out of place at one in the afternoon in the corridors of the White House.

"How?" Daniel guided her down a second flight of stairs that opened into a grand foyer. She'd seen this staircase, or a good replica, in far too many movies. The Grand Staircase was just that. A sweeping majesty trod by Annette Bening in a killer blue gown and great shoes. And now the real set of stairs bore Dr. Alice Thompson in garishly green sneakers and dirty corduroys.

Though she did have a killer handsome guy by her side, so it wasn't a complete loss. At least until she turned the corner of the stair. A long marble hall spread before them. A sea of gold-trimmed red carpet flowed down the marbled length as if it would never end. It was staggering, sunlight pouring in from tall windows made the room glow.

The room itself so dazzled the mind that it took her a moment to focus on the hoard of people at the far end of the hallway. Dozens and dozens of people, with a watchful phalanx of security guards, were stringing garlands, erecting and decorating trees, hanging dazzlingly intricate paper snowflakes several feet across from the ceiling using a high-lift platform.

"Christmas is here." Her voice had a sense of breathy wonder as if she were witnessing a modern miracle.

Daniel paused and looked out with her. "Four hundred volunteers. It will take them the better part of a day even at the rate they're moving. By this evening there will be musicians in the lobby, the whole bit."

He led her around the turn in the staircase as she rubbernecked like any tourist trying to take it all in. Right until she came face-to-face with Franklin D. Roosevelt, seated ever so grandly in a painted portrait almost as tall as she was.

It took her a moment to recover. Daniel almost had her turned toward the next set of descending stairs when her head cleared enough to spot the towering double doors. At the midpoint of the marbled foyer sufficiently spacious to hold a ballroom dance, the decorators hadn't reached them yet.

"Those are doors," she pointed. "And it is bright and sunny on the other side of them. They lead outside. Those," she paused for emphasis, "are doors."

"They are." He continued to coax her toward the set of descending stairs, ignoring her discovery.

"Well, I found them." She emphasized the "I" strongly and imagined herself discovering the North Pole.

"You did." He started down the next flight of steps and she was half tempted to call his bluff and leave through the lately-discovered doors. She'd need to think up what to name them if she were going to publish her findings.

"Do you know what's on the other side of those doors?" Daniel asked from where he'd paused three steps below her.

Alice wasn't really sure. Other than the now-famous Doors of Alice discovered by one Dr. Thompson while journeying through new and definitely strange lands, White House cartography wasn't exactly her thing. She could name the leaders of the hundred-and-ninety-three U.N. member nations and the three that weren't, draw a to-scale map of southwest Asia including every city with a population over twenty thousand and most of the clandestine weapon supply routes, on-or-off road. But what lay beyond those doors, not so much.

"What?" she demanded in a voice that echoed surprisingly in the long stairwell and attracted the attention of some of the closer decorators.

"Half of the capital's press corps is through those doors. We've had the new Egyptian President visiting this morning and he and President Matthews are finishing a photo op out on the North Portico at the moment. That's why we held back the decorating until after his visit."

"Oh. Right, he's a leader in the Muslim Brotherhood. Wouldn't be right." Alice tried to think of a good comeback, but it failed aborning. Maybe for the moment she'd leave herself in Daniel's hands and not explore the Famous Alice Doors. She followed him down the stairs and through the vaulted underground corridor they'd now entered, not one bit less grand than the main hallway upstairs, if not quite so flashy. No decorations here. At least not yet.

"Where did you get such nice hands?" *Where did she get such a stupid question?* But it was out there and now she'd have to live with it.

He held one up as if to inspect it as they once again passed through the Palm Room and along the West Colonnade. The decorators had definitely been here. Garlands of green pine spiraled up each of the columns, broad red ribbons wrapped between.

"My dad. I think I can blame my hands on him."

"Daniel Drake Darlington II?"

"What? No, that was Dad's idea of a joke, he's Johnny by the way. He thought it was funny. He'd found two Daniel Drakes in the family tree. One, an authentic Brit turned pioneer, who stumbled into the Tennessee wilderness in the early 1700s and never left. The second, a lieutenant in the Civil War, fought for the South. Died young and stupid, but left behind a pregnant farmer's wife who ran the place with an iron fist. Dad felt one a century was a good mark and realized that he'd better use the name in a hurry if he wanted to get it done in the 1900s. He added the 'third' just to be funny, I guess."

"So, you're a slaver."

"Born and bred."

Alice followed him past another set of Marines who opened yet another set of doors for them before they could get there.

"Should I worry?"

"Nah. You're not my type." His voice was pure tease.

"You're not mine either." She shot back. But it was wrong, on both sides. An awkward silence fell for a moment. She glanced sideways at him as they stepped past a pair of Marines and through a door. Then she faced forward and she squeaked.

It was all Alice could do.

She tried to speak, but all she could emit was another, equally ridiculous, high-pitched squeak.

A quick turn to retreat back out the door she'd just come in proved fruitless. The Marines had already closed it behind her. She turned reluctantly back to face the room. It was huge. Magnificently furnished. Washington, Lincoln, and JFK stared down at her from the wall. She couldn't say walls, because there was only one wall.

The room was oval.

Chapter 8

The President entered and shook Alice's hand a hearty good morning.

"Good afternoon, Dr. Thompson. You slept well I trust?"

Wholly unable to speak, she again managed little more than another puppy-dog limp handshake in response. The man must think her totally witless. He waved her toward the inevitable cluster of seating.

"Oval!" still rattled around in her brain like a ship lost at sea. Presidential portraits glowered down at her. The bloody Resolute desk, built from the timbers of the HMS *Resolute* anchored one end of the space and a large fireplace anchored the other. Nothing on television prepared her for the impact, for the sheer power of the room. It towered two stories tall, the Presidential Seal built into the center of the ceiling, mirrored by the one in the vast rug.

She dropped onto a couch. Far more comfortable than it looked. It would be a good slouching couch for watching a sappy movie, she resisted the urge to test that theory. As she'd half expected, the President and his Chief of Staff took the two armchairs. A small rosewood table separated her from Daniel. From its surface, a rather stumpy Christmas gnome considered her carefully. His open satchel sported a selection of cheerfully wrapped chocolates.

"I wanted a chance to speak with you before you left."

"Me?" She blinked hard, but remained clearly wide awake. The President didn't fade leaving a Cheshire Cat smile, and they were definitely still seated in the Oval Office. Or maybe Daniel was the Cheshire Cat for he too was smiling at her, though in apparent empathy, as if reading her complete discomfiture at finding herself on the wrong side of the looking glass.

"Yes, I'd like to ask for your professional assessment of the situation."

Her assessment? The situation? She checked her hands, but they looked normal-sized and clutched no little glass bottles or bits of half-nibbled mushroom. She really was here, in this room, with these two men.

"I'll try to help, Mr. President." She glanced over at Daniel, "It's not wearing off."

He shrugged and offered her a slightly crooked smile. "Don't tell him," he nodded towards President Matthews. "It will just make his ego even more unbearable knowing he has that effect on you."

The President ignored the comment. "Your Director at the CIA feels that the S.A.D. is the proper operational asset to deploy into this situation. He states that the Special Activities Division can extract and reinsert personnel with the lowest statistical probability of detection. Quite adamant on that point in fact."

She would bet Director Smith was adamant. To have end-to-end control of such a high profile situation would be a distinct feather in the agency's cap.

"I also spoke with the Chairman of the Joint Chiefs. Brett was former commander of the U.S. Special Operations Command. As former head of SOCOM, he has an equally adamant predisposition favoring the SOAR assets. I'd like an analyst's opinion. Director Smith speaks very highly of your acumen in these situations."

"Something he is careful not to voice in my presence."

"A bit taciturn, but an exceptional man for the role."

Alice couldn't argue.

" 'She possesses,' " the President intoned in a fair imitation of Director Smith's voice, "the finest operational instinct the agency has seen in a dozen years.' I'd like to hear what your instinct says on this one."

Those were certainly words she'd never heard from the Director. In point of fact, over the six years since she'd first met the Director, that might be as many words as she'd ever heard from him, total. But that didn't help her much in the Oval Office.

Maybe if she could find a flagon of something that could make her shrink enough to completely disappear, then she'd feel much, much better.

Shape up, Alice. You've been studying for this moment since you first played the Take Off! *board game at age six, and then stayed up all night to memorize the country data on every single playing card.*

"Fact," good place to start. "We have a tentative contact requesting an extraction and subsequent reinsertion of a single individual out of and back into North Korea. Fact, as odd as this request appears on the outside, if certain recent changes following Kim Jong-il's death are considered, a certain logic may be conjectured." She wished she had a white board. She always did her best thinking with a white board.

She closed her eyes for a moment to let the patterns of the last three days of research reintegrate in her thinking. Then opened them again. They both still waited quietly. Well, she couldn't ask for a more attentive audience.

"Straight-line conclusions—"

"What does that mean in analyst-speak?"

"It means, Mr. President, that the only reasonable conclusions I can draw from the existing data lead straight to a single set of conclusions. Each change of factors decreases the scenario likelihood, significant decreases in this case. In other words, no matter what other geo-political influences I consider, I can only see one conclusion that makes any sense without stretching into impossible realms. And as my buddy, Sherlock says…"

"Sherlock?"

"Holmes, sir," Daniel completed for her. " 'Once you have eliminated the obvious, whatever remains, no matter how improbable, must be the truth.' "

It was like they'd been thinking together for years, the thoughts just flowed. Daniel just kept getting sexier. To get some distance, she stood and walked toward the far end of the room.

"My dear Daniel Watson is quite correct." She winced at her insertion of the word "dear" but forged ahead. The fireplace mantel had been adorned with a splendid collection of homey items, though she'd bet this was the White House staff's doing, not some volunteers. Maybe even the President's; this one little group of decorations looked age-worn and personal.

Red-and-white candy-cane-twist candles. A little set of brass angels poised to ring tiny brass bells. A heavy iron strap sporting three very old bells the size of the palm of her hand. She picked it up and gave it a shake. Sleigh bells! Real ones. They clanged merrily and echoed loudly about the room reminding her of the auspicious place where she stood.

She put the bells down hastily and turned back to the room. She couldn't approach the problem head on, she always had to come at problems a bit sideways. So, she followed the wall past a grandfather clock and a curved door, the same shape as the wall.

"The only thing that fits the data is that a high-ranking official of the North Korean government wishes to have an unofficial conversation with an equal member of the United States government. The trip must be a secret, hence the unofficial channels of the request and the request of non-North Korean transport." She moseyed past the doors with a hazed view of the backs of the Marine guards, the glass so thick that it blurred the light. People shot bullets at this room. She shivered and hurried by only to be faced with Lincoln glaring at her from the ever-present oval wall. To his left stood a Christmas tree so perfect that it belonged in a catalog, not in real life. No family ornaments, no little kid decorations. A bachelor's Christmas tree set up by others.

"It must be a high-ranking official, one with sufficient profile to be recognized if traveling via normal transport. Hence, the request for clandestine transport. Perhaps even to be missed if gone overlong." She whistled. She'd missed that. "Top six, at least that's how I think of them. One of four leaders of the major political organizations: Central Committee, the Presidium, Worker's Assembly, or National Defense. Or perhaps one of the two people who make up the ruling triumvirate with Kim Jong-un: Sung-il or Pak."

She ducked under Lincoln's gaze and returned to the fireplace and its Christmas-bedecked marble mantelpiece. The room wasn't actually that big, about the size of her whole apartment. Looking up she saw that a very solemn George Washington inspected her closely. This place was crazy. The first President's steady gaze finally drove her back to face the current President's thoughtful expression.

"A three-day extraction, which means they'd be missed if they were gone longer. And they don't want to be missed. They don't want to be noticed as having anything to do with the Wicked West.

"They aren't stupid. They know it will take three days. Two days in transit, out and back in, and one day on the ground. The request mandates neutral territory. Neither China, Russia, Japan, nor the United States. We have three weeks to arrange a location, set and rehearse the extraction, and execute. And it must be flawless or the whole thing comes apart."

She sat back down, her throat dry from talking. Daniel had poured her a cup of tea in a delicate, holly-painted cup, and rested it on the small table between them. She'd never even seen him go to the sideboard. She took the lemon, careful not to spray the table or sofa arm, but didn't add any sugar.

"Special Activities Division?" The President reminded her.

She considered the pieces. Knew the profiles of Saul and his crew, the best the CIA had in helicraft. Nothing else could perform this operation but a helicopter. There was no way to fly a comfy passenger- or military-jet into North Korea, twice, yet remain undetected. Saul had certainly done some nasty missions and come out with his crew and his cargo intact.

"It must be one of the Top Six." She whispered it aloud, even capitalizing it in her mind though there was no so-named group, to test the sound of the hypothesis. Unless it was… No, that theory didn't quite work. Still, the factors didn't block it. No! It was too ludicrous to consider. Certainly too unlikely to voice in this room or to this company.

"Top Six," she said it definitively and knew it was right. Most likely. Now she focused back on her audience.

"Beyond secrecy, this mission will require finesse. The S.A.D. assets could do it. But if a North Korean Top Six asset caught the least little whiff of CIA involvement, or the attitude those fliers tend to carry with them, they'll be gone. Never come aboard. No, you need a SOAR operative. One with the kind of finesse I've seen on Beale and Henderson's reports. I'd trust your first instinct when you called them in last night." And with that simple assessment, she'd probably just cancelled out every nice thing the CIA Director had ever thought about her.

Chapter 9

Daniel escorted Alice along the underground corridor to where her car had been moved and parked beneath the Treasury Building. A valet had it rolled up to the door, heater already running against the December chill.

"Thank you, Daniel. It would have been just too weird walking through all of that security alone." She glanced back through the glass doors at the last of three security desks they'd passed. Designed to keep people from getting in, it also made sure that she retained nothing important on her way out.

"Always glad to serve as your Dear Daniel Watson."

Damn! She really hadn't meant for it to come out that way, though of course he'd caught it. So, she did her best to smile in response.

He held her car door for her, shooing the valet off with a five-dollar bill. By the boy's expression, Alice could see that tips weren't really called for, but he was being so overeager and helpful Daniel properly assessed it was the only way he could have a final private moment with her.

Alice found herself not minding a private moment in the least.

"I have a meeting tonight, but do you have plans for tomorrow evening?"

She found herself shaking her head even before she could think as to whether or not she really did.

"Good. I'll come get you at 7pm. Casual."

Her first thought, as she tried to tug her cardigan more tightly around her, was there was no way she'd ever again risk wearing casual around Daniel Drake Darlington III. Her second thought was that she couldn't wait.

He clicked the door closed behind her, the closed window cutting off any chance of a response.

It was only after she was driving away, and she spotted him still watching her departure, that she felt the warmth where his hand had brushed down her cheek before he'd closed her door.

Chapter 10

By midnight Alice had convinced herself that she'd imagined the whole thing, especially the line of warmth she could still feel on her cheek.

By one o'clock she was pretty sure she hadn't, and around two a.m. she decided she'd better be ready in case he actually came for her.

Sometime around three she'd finally passed out for four hours of shuteye.

By ten the next morning she'd dropped a significant portion of her next paycheck on a killer dress and new shoes. That had required a new winter coat to avoid looking totally ridiculous; can't wear a killer dress with a worn blue parka. She'd had her hair cut just last week, the only reason she didn't go in and have something drastic done to "fix" herself. Even in the salon, her hair had never behaved, though how she wish it would just for one night.

To get over herself, she swung by the office and dove into her own analysis. Her premise, try to prove it wrong. If she couldn't, well, then she had even more thinking to do. She reviewed the last six months of news from the incredibly spotlight-shy communist nation and its equally elusive leadership. Nothing revealed a softening to their strict isolationist attitudes. No comment reported by any of North Korea's Top Six gave the least hint of who was coming out or what they'd want to talk about. The new supreme leader, Kim Jong-un, now named Wonsu, the highest active military rank, provided no indication of any change to his deceased father's paranoid policies.

When Betsy asked if she was coming to S.A.D. training or not, Alice observed the time in shock. Six o'clock. She locked down her work and was out of the building before Betsy could repeat the question. Thankfully no cops waited along the two-mile drive to her apartment.

A shower and fast change.

The dress was nearly impossible to zip up by herself, but she managed, thankful for the flexibility gained in the S.A.D. gymnasium.

Her nose shone, despite powder. Her cheeks didn't, despite a bit of blush.

Disgusted with the whole effort, she washed it all off her face and accidentally dribbled water down her cleavage. The dress hadn't seemed so revealing in the store. She had just managed her shoes, a mid-heels compromise, as a knock sounded on the door. A quick glance proved that there was no way she was letting Daniel into her apartment in its current state.

The couch had a rumpled afghan she'd knit years ago to snuggle under while watching movies, a fair pile of which she hadn't filed away. A stack of books covered much of the armchair she didn't use. Her home computer and a friendly disarray of paper, projects, and empty teacups scattered about the surface of the dining table. With a quick kick, at least the clothes she'd stripped and dumped on arriving home would be out of sight.

Coat. That was it. Be completely ready to leave. She snagged the knee-length wrap-around black cashmere coat. She overlapped it and tugged the wide belt tight around her waist. She liked that it had made her look like a modern secret agent in the store mirror.

She opened the door just as the knock repeated.

It wasn't Daniel.

She didn't manage to suppress either her surprise or her disappointment.

"Dr. Thompson?" The man was big, crew cut, mid-forties. The kind of square features you wouldn't want to mess with. The incongruous black suit looked distinctly out of place on his fighter's frame despite the good fit. The small coiled wire leading to an earpiece marked him for what he was, an agent of the U.S. Secret Service.

"Uh, I'm she." Lame! "I'm Alice, er, Doctor, uh. Oh crap! Yea, that's me."

"Frank Adams, ma'am." He didn't even blink at her being a total idiot. "Sorry that I'm a disappointment, but Dr. Darlington was unable to get away. He didn't want to be late, so he asked if I could come and provide you with transportation."

"Oh, okay." Alice had hoped to wow Daniel with her new look, and instead she was suddenly facing one of the President's personal bodyguards. The shift was jarring.

"May I say ma'am, that if I weren't married, I'd be even more sorry that I'm a disappointment. You look great."

"Uh, thanks." That gave Alice some hope of not appearing like a total frump.

"Though, if I may?"

She shrugged her permission.

With a move that she barely registered despite her S.A.D. training, the massive man suddenly held a short, but nasty looking knife to her wrist. Before she could protest, he gave it a practiced flick and then it disappeared again from view.

With his other hand he offered her the price tag that had been dangling from the coat sleeve.

Chapter 11

Daniel met her at the garlanded North Portico, the very entrance Alice had discovered the day before. Now she knew what lay on both sides of the Doors of Alice. Daniel opened the car door himself and handed her out.

"I thought you said, 'casual'." She admired the charcoal gray suit that revealed a breadth of shoulder unusual for an office worker. Of course she knew why. Yesterday, wow, was it just yesterday, she'd woken earlier than Daniel thought and had gone out in hunt of food on the top floor of the White House Residence.

Instead of the kitchen, Alice had stumbled on the small gym where Daniel, clad in only shorts and sneakers, had laid on a bench pumping iron while watching CNN. And she'd thought he was gorgeous clothed.

She'd headed back to her room and waited for her nerves to settle before returning, by which time he was showered, dressed, and eating lunch. She'd had a terrible time meetings his eyes as she ate her yogurt for fear he'd see the truth in her face. The truth of what even being in the same room with Daniel made her feel.

"I had different plans, more casual plans," Daniel apologized as he led her inside. "There's a quiet little fish house I was going to take you to, but South Africa happened and we've only just wrapped it up. We'll just have a quiet dinner in the Residence."

Alice slowed to a halt as the door shushed closed behind her. The broad marble hall of yesterday morning had been transformed into a winter fairyland. The giant paper snowflakes of impossible intricacy dangled down the entire length of the Entrance and Cross Halls on the first floor of the Residence. A spray of glitter and subtle lighting had made them glow; the sole source of light in the hall. Columns of ice, she tapped one, plastic, flowed from floor to ceiling as if they held up the snowflake sky.

In sparkling contrast, a massive Christmas tree shone through the open double-doors ahead of her.

Daniel took her arm and coaxed her forward, "The Blue Room Christmas Tree. The room is just a little bigger than the Oval Office. This is only the second year since Jackie Kennedy that there hasn't been a First Lady to decorate it." Last year and this year. Following the death of First Lady Katherine Matthews.

Alice could only stare. It soared magnificently. A thousand ornaments must dangle from its limbs. Industry. It took her a moment, but that was clearly the theme. All of the ornaments had been made from a warm, dusky metal; pewter and bronze. Tiny airplanes, trains, automobiles, ships, and hundreds of other familiar objects had been created with a perfection and grace.

Each ornament lit by a pair of tiny Christmas lights in a vast rainbow of colors. She'd always favored using only white lights, but this tree could convert her to the many-hued camp.

The deep blue walls had been lit like the night sky, tiny sparkles making the room appear boundless. It was breathtaking.

Daniel allowed her to look to her heart's content before leading her up the Grand Staircase.

She kept her secret agent coat firmly wrapped around her as he led up to the second story and down to massive central hallway. The decorators had been here as well. A couple of cheery Christmas trees made the long hall homey. Wreaths bedecked the doors and someone with an immense amount of patience had woven overlapping red-and-green ribbons in a spiral about each column. Everything here was designed to make her feel small, but tonight she was simply going to refuse. Somehow.

"This is the President's personal living room," he turned for an open doorway.

"I thought you said a quiet dinner in the residence?" Somehow, she'd pictured the two of them back in the cozy brass and cherry wood kitchen on the third floor. Just the two of them.

"Just the President."

"Do I look like the President?" A female voice sounded from past Daniel's shoulder where he'd half-turned to speak to her.

Alice didn't need the reminder of the midnight video conference to identify the first female pilot of SOAR. Major Emily Beale was dressed casually in ACUs, but made it look formal. The Army Combat Uniform had golden oak leaves that shone on the collar points of her blouse. That's all that was needed to dress her formally. The long, slender, perfectly-formed blonde was so stunning she could probably make rags appear elegant.

Alice, as the queen of frump, didn't need to be reminded of the fact by having to be in the same room with this woman. Sure thing no one would be paying her any attention tonight. Which normally was fine with her, but tonight it bothered her.

"Major Mark Henderson." Beale's husband came into view as Alice fully entered the room. His handshake was solid and friendly. He'd have stood out in any room that didn't contain his wife. Or Daniel.

"Dr. Alice Thompson," she managed a decent handshake this time.

"CIA analyst Dr. Alice Thompson?" Major Beale who hadn't even bothered to shake her hand now inspected her carefully with a full attention so complete that Alice almost stumbled backward.

"You did the report last year on that new arms route they were developing southeast of Asadabad?"

Alice nodded. That had been three months of her life.

"You'll be glad to know that your information let us wipe the hell out of it. If they even think about trying it again, we'll own their asses. Well done."

Major Beale's simple nod may have been the highest praise Alice had ever received in her life. The woman was clearly a primal force. If she'd thought it was a load of crap, Alice would bet she'd have said as much.

"That is good to know. Thank you."

"Yep!" Major Henderson wrapped an arm around his wife's waist and pulled her tight against him. "We cruised up there just last week or so; all part of our full inspection and on-going maintenance service. Whole sections of that pass don't even exist anymore. Seems that some significant chunks of the road disappeared off the cliff face and wound up in the valley a few thousand feet below. Can't imagine how that happened."

Alice could tell just by the immensely self-satisfied tone in Henderson's voice. A dozen Hellfire missiles here. Call into the Air Force for a bunker-buster bomb there. No more Kunar-Bajaur Link Road. The Taliban had moved a million or more dollars of ammunition across that pass last year alone, wholesale. Nice to know that had stopped.

# # #

Daniel took Alice's coat and turned to hang it up in the closet.

"Holy shit!" he heard the President's deep voice.

Daniel spun to see what had caused a President, who didn't even swear at midnight wakeup calls, to curse.

His eyes quickly passed over the occupants of the room and almost made it to where the President stood stock still at the door to his private bedroom. But Daniel didn't quite get there. A sight dragged his attention back to the woman whose coat even now slipped from his numb fingers and cascaded about his feet.

Cream skin and russet curls had been offset by a sleeveless green sheath dress so dark and rich that it made one understand what Mother Nature had been striving for when she'd designed the leaves of a holly tree. It draped left over right in a cascade that appeared to flow from one of Alice's shoulders, the other exquisitely uncovered. Not a curve of her body missed or hidden, but neither overemphasized. It was perhaps the most elegant dress he had ever seen.

Then Alice turned those hazel eyes on him and, though her skin had flushed red, that amazing smile lit her face.

"You appear to have dropped my coat, Dr. Darlington."

He looked at his feet indeed lost in a puddle of black cashmere, but he couldn't think of what to do about it. All he could do was look back at the woman.

The President came up and thumped him hard in the center of his back driving what little air remained out of his lungs. "Breathe, man. Breathe before you pass out."

Daniel gasped and suddenly felt quite lightheaded as his body dragged in desperately needed air.

The President retrieved the coat from about Daniel's feet. As he rose, he leaned in and offered in a loud whisper that anyone could here. "Speak, man. At least tell her how nice she looks."

He tried, he really did.

Then he cursed, spun, and strode from the room.

# # #

Alice stood frozen by his abrupt and apparently furious departure. Had he been upset that she'd dressed nicely when he said casual? She fought against tears when Emily hissed in her ear.

"If he's what you want, go! Move, damn it!"

Alice was out of the room and down the hall before she had time to chicken out.

Alice caught up with Daniel at the far end of the Central Hall where he'd come to a stop against a grand piano. He clutched the edge of case like a man drowning.

"Do you play?" she did her best to ask, to make it light and funny, but she couldn't be sure that the words actually escaped past the tension that throttled her throat.

He nodded. Didn't speak. Didn't turn. Just a nod.

Alice couldn't do it. Whatever momentum had carried her this far was gone. She felt drained. Once again she'd proven her mother's words right, no one would ever want her. No one ever had, except for maybe a quick tumble and an equally quick goodbye. She was always too smart or not pretty enough or who the hell knew. By twenty-seven you think she'd be smart enough to know that men like the White House Chief of Staff would never want her to be anything other than meek and mild. A neatly classifiable object.

Well, she was better than that. She hadn't spoken to her mother for the last five years the woman had been alive for a reason. Self-preservation. Well, that too was a hard won lesson. Her best option was to go. Now.

Her eyes hot and stinging, she turned to leave. Maybe she could find that Secret Service agent who'd brought her and go home. Or maybe not. The building was as hard to get out of as it was to get into.

"Wait." His voice, barely a whisper, drifted down the hall.

"Why?" She stood with her back to him, no more than a half dozen steps between them.

"Please?"

So she stood. Stood and started counting to thirty. At thirty, to hell with what he wanted, she would leave anyway.

At twenty-two, she felt a fingertip brush ever so slightly across the bare shoulder. Rather than a shiver, a ring of warmth radiated from that brief contact.

Paralyzed, she couldn't turn to face him.

Another brush of fingers and he caught some of her tears where they'd run unnoticed down her cheek.

"This is going to sound wrong."

"It's got to be better than silence."

She could half see him nod in her peripheral vision, but she refused to turn. The silence was killing her.

"I don't want it to be about the physical."

"It?" she asked. "You're so good with words, use them now when it matters."

Again the peripheral nod.

Alice's eyes focused down the hall. A pair of Secret Service agents stood outside the room where she could hear the others talking. Twenty paces away, they were clearly trying to not pay attention to the drama unfolding over by the piano.

"Will you sit, please?"

At her nod, he led her a little farther down the hall from the agents to a pair of armchairs placed close in friendly companionship. A small metallic tree dangling with dozens of tiny ball ornaments graced the small table.

She sat carefully, remembering she was wearing a gown and not corduroy slacks. Alice inspected her own hands. Could just see Daniel's where they were folded together. There was a similarity that she could now identify, why his hands had looked particularly nice to her. They both had pianist's muscles, a strength that came from the constant practice.

Again that crazy-making silence.

"You were going to define the 'it' you were talking about."

"Right." He took a deep breath and puffed it back out. "Right."

She considered pointing out that he was repeating himself rather than making any headway, but she was afraid that would just earn her another "right" and she'd probably scream if he did that.

"I have all of these stupid ideas."

"What kind of ideas? And don't say stupid ones. I've heard that bit already."

"Right—"

"Or 'Right.' I've had enough of that word too."

Daniel reached out and took her hands. Somehow that forced her to look up into his brilliant blue eyes.

"You, in that dress, are the most beautiful thing I've ever seen."

"Thing?" she managed to give her brain a moment to shift gears, but it wasn't enough. She knew she could pass for cute, but "most beautiful?" Not likely.

"Yes. Yes, for crying out loud! 'Most beautiful woman,' while nonetheless true, is far too small a category."

"Oh." Her voice was small, even she could barely hear it.

"I always believed that attraction should be built on a mutual respect, two minds that find similar interests. On the rare occasions when I have dated—"

"How rare?" The question popped out of the cataloging side of her mind.

"Rare enough. On those occasions, I've always grown to know the woman well before I, before we, before…" He huffed out a breath in exasperation, glanced over toward the two agents down the hall and then lowered his voice and leaned a little closer until she could truly see the amazing purity of blue in his eyes, no hints of brown at all.

"I'm so sorry I kissed you."

"Why? Why are you sorry, Daniel?" She'd liked it so much.

"Because it was inappropriate. I did it just because I wanted you so much I couldn't stop myself. It's a lousy excuse and it won't happen again, but I have no better—"

She leaned the last few inches and stopped his words with her lips. She ran her fingers up into the soft blond hair and dug them in so that he couldn't pull back without taking her with him.

Daniel held off for the longest moment, then groaned and leaned in. His hands slipped along her cheeks and gentle thumbs rubbed along her ears. He kissed her so long and deep that she practically felt ravaged. She'd had sex that was less meaningful. Actually, Alice would wager that she'd never had sex that was anywhere near as meaningful as this kiss.

When at last he released her lips, he didn't move away, but remained forehead-to-forehead, nose tip-to-nose tip.

"If you say you're sorry, I'm going to smack you."

"Then," his whisper matched hers, "I won't. I've dreamed of nothing else but kissing you again since when I kissed you goodnight the first time. And maybe before that."

"Well, if you behave, maybe I'll let you kiss me goodnight tonight, too." If her heart could stand it.

He rose from the chair and helped her to her feet, which was good because her knees were distinctly watery and the mid-height heels were proving more precarious than planned. She and Daniel headed back to join the others, the pair of agents studiously inspecting the wall across the hall from the doorway they guarded. It was only as they reentered the room that she realized that Daniel had not released her hand from when he'd helped her to her feet.

Just the moment before anyone noticed their return, she leaned close and whispered quietly in Daniel's ear.

"I've been thinking about a lot more than just kissing you."

Chapter 12

Daniel sat at his desk the next morning and ignored the piles of paper that had grown significantly overnight.

He couldn't help smiling at the memory of that moment last night in the President's living room. For the second time in a dozen minutes, President Matthews had been required to slap Daniel's back and remind him to breathe. Over cocktails, they divided pretty typically along gender lines, but for atypical reasons.

The men often stopped to join in on the women's conversation. They appeared to have become instant long lost friends and the energy of it was electrifying. They were long lost friends who were both fascinated with the ebb and flow of global military tactics as they swept back and forth across the planet. Emily and Mark had amazing insights into the variations of localized conflict and the shifting tactics in the actual theater of operations.

Daniel offered country-level insights, and the President posited some fascinating cultural-level aspects in understanding some of the conflicts and their global ramifications that Daniel hadn't previously considered.

Again, it was Dr. Alice who startled and amazed. She backed up her beauty with a very serious mind. She followed Mark and Emily into actual battlefield tactics that completely eluded Daniel even when they tried to explain them. At the same time, she was able to expand his and the President's thinking on several subjects. When questioned, she backed up her comments with facts.

53

As their small party shifted and regrouped into different conversations, first in the living room and later around the dining table, he never managed to remove her from his awareness. That this breathtaking woman had been thinking about a lot more than kissing him had now rooted his thoughts there as well. He tried to imagine helping her out of that dress.

It was a thought he definitely enjoyed. But he couldn't quite picture it. Whereas making love to her dressed only in that well-worn cardigan sweater, that he could picture just fine. As if that were the real Alice, and last night's stunning and brilliant beauty in the perfect evening gown who had radiated as the center of the evening, she was someone he'd never deserve.

Suddenly his desk phone rang from somewhere under the latest Mexico currency crisis. The drug cartels had hinted that they were going to wholly abandon the peso in favor of the more stable U.S. dollar. The news had crashed the peso's valuation badly. Again.

"Daniel."

"You aren't opening today's Advent calendar window are you?"

"Good morning, Dr. Thompson." He pulled the calendar into his lap and opened to the first picture.

"Did you? No cheating or mama would know."

"No cheating. As a matter of fact, thoughts of you so distracted me last night that I haven't even opened December 2nd's window and today is the third. You distract me, Dr. Thompson."

"Bad luck."

"Your distracting me?"

"Not opening the window. Do it now, I'll wait."

He pulled on the "2" ribbon, attached to a little flap door in the snow at the base of a tree. He pulled out the butterscotch drop and admired a pair of squirrels sleeping curled up inside. The sides of the little space had been painted with tiny cupboards. One open cabinet revealed a bountiful stock of acorns.

He described it to her.

"Hmm," she hummed in his ear. "Butterscotch. I'll bet you taste good with butterscotch."

"I really didn't need that image stuck in my head all day."

"Tough," her laugh sparkled even over the phone line.

"When can I see you again? I have to see if you taste as luscious in normal clothes as you did in that amazing dress." Their full-body goodnight kiss had almost led him to throw her over his shoulder and drag her upstairs to his bedroom.

"Hmm," she hummed at him again. "I'll pick you up this time. Eight o'clock. Eat first, dress warm."

"Hmm," he hummed back at her. Sounded stupid when he did it. He glanced up to see Janet standing across his desk holding a couple of files.

Clearly she made a similar assessment about the inefficacy his hmm-ing ability.

"Tonight at eight." He tried to sound business-like.

"Janet just walked in, didn't she?" That merry giggle sounded in his ear. "Tell her I said hi."

"Will do." Not a chance. He hung up the phone.

Chapter 13

"I considered sending an agent to pick you up, but came myself instead."

Alice always seemed to start conversations without any preamble. Daniel didn't even have both feet inside her fire-engine red Prius yet. It had flames painted on the front like a 1960s GTO muscle car instead of a mundane hybrid. A cheery little garland of tiny red-and-green lights glowed softly around the rear view mirror.

She headed them back out the White House gates.

Maybe it was his Tennessee background, but conversations had a normal flow, a way they were supposed to work. A greeting, a checking in, those pleasant little inanities that served no purpose he could put his finger on at the moment, but he liked them nonetheless. It wasn't as if she was in a hurry, she was simply always in forward motion and he always lagged a step behind.

"I did apologize for sending an agent to pick you up."

"Sent me home with one, too."

"I…" He had. Hadn't even thought about it. He was so used to the building, it seemed that he never left it except for meetings up on the Hill.

He'd moved into the White House Residence when Peter Matthews had made him the Chief of Staff. "Every time you leave for your apartment, you're going to lose another half-hour of sleep between walking to your car, driving, parking." So, he'd kept the apartment for a while, but finally moved fully into the third floor of the Residence. With Katherine Matthews dead in the helicopter crash, that had left President

Matthews living alone in the entire Residence. Daniel had felt sorry for him and did really appreciate the man's company when they could stop moving long enough to enjoy a gathering like last night.

Daniel had never given a thought to delivering her home himself. In hindsight, it would have been a very dangerous choice, vastly increasing the likelihood of his ending up in her bed. But last night, he'd been too dazed by her goodnight kiss to form any coherent thoughts.

"What did Janet put in the calendar for tonight?"

Apparently his silence had lasted too long. She cleared the gate and turned south.

"I don't know. I didn't look."

"Don't you get the rules at all, Dr. Darlington? It's after dark. There are rules to these things."

"Rules like not pulling over so that I can drag you into the tall grass and neck wildly like two teenagers?"

The car actually wavered on the road and he reached out a steadying hand to the wheel for a moment.

"Well," she cleared her throat and tried again. "Well, being early December, the tall grass has long since been mown by the Parks Department and died back for the winter. Otherwise that sounds like a great idea."

Now it was his turn to try and speak. It took him several tries.

"I'm new to Advent calendar rules, but I'm learning. I brought it with me."

"Well, that's better. So open it already!" She turned onto the Frederick Douglass bridge and crossed south over the river. Still no word where she was taking him and he wasn't going to ask.

He pulled the calendar out of his bag that also included a hat and mittens. By the light of the street lights strobing by overhead, he found the "3" ribbon, a small, gift-wrapped present that an owl had dropped in the snow and was in the process of retrieving.

"Black licorice. A Scotty dog."

"Ooo. They're the best."

He plucked it out and another lay behind it. Two Scotty dogs. Had Janet originally given him two? Or had she somehow discerned he had a date and slipped in the second one while the calendar lay on his desk? He'd rather think the former, but suspected the later.

"Here, there's two." He held one out so she could take it with her teeth. She did so, nibbling on the ends of his fingers in the process.

He was suddenly glad he wasn't driving or they'd be weaving all over the road.

He popped in his own and started chewing.

"That's so good," she mumbled. "I need to stop and see how you taste." And she did. Turned into a side road, parked, and leaned over.

He met her halfway. Winter and summer and sweet licorice. Unable to stop himself, he reached for her, and to the limits of the seatbelts, pulled their bodies together, one hand running down over her coat, tracing the many-layered curve of her breast making Alice moan against his teeth.

A sharp knock on the window made him open his eyes. A Marine in full uniform was leaning down to inspect them through the driver's window. Where had he come from?

Chapter 14

"Anacostia?" Daniel had waited until the Marine cleared them through the gate. Obviously they'd been expected. "What the hell are we doing at Anacostia? The only thing here are Marine helicopters used to transport the President."

"Not the only thing." Alice was clearly enjoying whatever little secret she had. What else could possibly be here?

"Hey, who are these guys who keep following us?" Alice was checking the rearview mirror.

Daniel didn't even bother to glance back. "Secret Service. They're my protection detail."

"Since when?"

"Since the day Katherine Matthews' helicopter was shot down and I became Chief of Staff."

"No, I mean when tonight? It was shot down?"

"Yes." Daniel had heard enough to know gunfire had been involved in the final, fatal crash. He still wondered what had truly happened on that final flight. No one was telling him and he'd decided that discretion was the better part of curiosity and never tried to pull the file for study. If there even was a file. It had been a very strange three weeks while Emily Beale was working undercover in the White House.

"Emily Beale," he finally connected the pieces. "She's here at Anacostia. With her helicopter." He groaned. "Please tell me we're not going flying."

"Absolutely! She called to invite me this morning and I can't wait. It's gonna be great!" Her excitement was contagious, or would be under other circumstances. He'd seen Emily fly only five or six times in those three weeks and she'd crashed during two of them. Not odds that he liked even if he knew the reasons for the first one. He'd been there and survived only because of her amazing skills. But still, they'd crashed.

"So how long have they been following us tonight?"

Funny, Alice might start in the middle of conversations, but she never lost their thread once begun.

"Since the White House gates."

She went silent at that as she pulled up into the parking spot by a hangar door.

"You live like that?"

"Part of the job."

She went quiet again.

Daniel had to acknowledge, it could be a shocking price to pay. The loss of personal privacy in trade for a measure of security against being murdered by some nutcase.

If this attraction between them built into something more, would it be a price Alice could stand to pay?

Chapter 15

"We have two flights tonight." Major Beale indicated the two helicopters parked inside the hangar. Alice tried to get her clothes to settle properly. They'd given her a flight suit that covered her from collar to boots. The vest added another layer. Daniel wore a similar rig and managed to make it look enticing; like you'd want to strip it off to see what lay beneath. She felt like a balloon animal.

The black-painted Black Hawk bristled with armament and radar domes. It had to be the DAP version. She'd never actually seen one of SOAR's notorious Direct Action Penetrator modifications. No one else flew these. There were perhaps twenty of them in existence and it was the nastiest and most effective piece of airborne weaponry ever launched into the night sky.

It looked modern, cruel, and impossibly deadly.

The other helicopter was almost a joke beside it. She'd seen a thousand pictures of the Mil's Mi-4 "Hound." The first true workhorse Russian helicopter by Mikhail Mil. Over three thousand had been built. So ubiquitous and stubbornly tough that a number of countries still flew them, though the last new one had come off the line in 1964. Based on the American 1950s-era Sikorsky S-55, it looked completely out of place besides its cousin, the Sikorsky Black Hawk MH-60M.

Alice didn't have to ask what it was doing here; the idea had a brilliance in its simplicity. Emily nodded to her, acknowledging Alice's quick understanding.

Beale and Henderson could enter North Korea in one of two different ways. On board the DAP Hawk they would have speed, night-vision, and nap-of-earth flying capabilities making them as nearly invisible as any weapon of war could become.

If they flew into the country with the Mi-4, they'd also be near enough invisible for a different reason. North Korea still used them as military trainers and agricultural birds. One of the last dozen countries to do so. No one would think twice about seeing one. But the mission would give up speed, maneuverability, and any chance of taking drastic action if called for.

"A tough choice," Alice acknowledged.

"Mark and I have been back and forth on it." Emily scowled at the two birds as if it were their fault. "We're doing simulated missions in each tonight, hoping that will help answer the question. They're the same weight, but the Hawk has half again the speed, twice the range, and four times the power. Should be interesting."

Alice had already learned that in Emily Beale's world, "interesting" was a word indicating a complete and all-consuming fascination. The mistress of understatement, nothing was more important to the Major than helicopters and especially the task at hand.

"Let's start with the Hawk," Alice suggested. "That's your familiar ground, your baseline. Set your calibration point and then reference variations from there."

Emily nodded agreement and waved a hand toward the Black Hawk.

Several things happened from that simple gesture. A couple of men Alice hadn't previously noticed back in the shadows moved forward and began working over the DAP Hawk. These would be her crew chiefs, a mismatched pair.

One no taller than Alice but exceptionally broad-shouldered and slim-waisted, a six-pack ab kind of guy. The other was a huge man. Not an ounce that wasn't muscle, but tall and wide. If he played a hockey goalie, no one would ever see the net past his bulk. They moved over the bird with the ease of long practice and the silence of long familiarity. A good team.

"We dropped in a couple of observer seats for you." Emily indicated the back of the cargo bay. Two seats had been added, just like the ones for the gunners, low because of the four-foot height of the cargo bay. A circle of red-and-green Christmas lights had been arranged around the back of the pilots' seats lending a cheery glow to the cabin.

"That's great. I love it. Thanks." Alice wondered if she could tease the woman, always worth a try. "Daniel says you like to crash a lot."

Emily offered the slightest smile. "Well, we'll see if we can keep tonight's mishaps limited to just the simulated ones."

Alice nodded, just as upright and forthright as she'd expected.

Then Emily offered her a beatific smile. "But don't tell Daniel it's only practice."

Alice laughed.

Chapter 16

The Black Hawk ride had been everything Alice had imagined. They took off low and fast and roared down the Potomac as if they were racing over the Sea of Japan. A winter storm on the Atlantic had kicked up wind and whitecaps on the Chesapeake Bay. The chopper bumped and dropped in the wind while they flew so low it looked as if the waves were going to claw them from out of the sky.

With a hard slam, they tilted nearly sideways and turned overland. They flew so low that they actually had to bounce upward to clear fences. The silence on the radio was absolute. The heavy helmets they wore offering only the slightest hiss over the built-in headphones to indicate they were latched into the radio and intercom system at all.

Alice could see the infrared projection of the FLIR across the inside of her visor, passed to her by the nose-mounted forward-looking-infrared camera. It revealed trees with alarming suddenness as they traveled over the Virginia countryside at just under two hundred miles an hour.

"Pending engine failure," Mark Henderson announced from the left seat with a calmness that was startling, even in a practice scenario.

"Oh no!" Daniel's whisper. "Not again."

Alice had heard Emily tell the rest of the crew that they wouldn't say the word "simulated" on this flight. Everyone was in the know but Daniel.

He convulsively clutched Alice's hand.

"Silence on the intercom," Beale snapped out. "Roger failure on one and two. Restart check."

"Restart failure on one and two."

"Roger. Initiating auto-rotate emergency landing."

Alice's could feel the adrenaline pounding her heart against her rib cage as the bird backed hard in a nose-high position to shed their forward speed. The ground was so close.

Alice bit the inside of her cheek hard enough that for a moment she'd thought she'd drawn blood. If she felt this stressed, even knowing it was a test, she now felt awful for pulling the trick on Daniel. But she didn't dare speak while the pilots were so busy "saving" them. So instead she did her best to calmly pat his arm.

At the last moment, with the ground barely a dozen feet away, but still moving forward quickly, Emily did something and the rotor blades dropped into silence. The helicopter fell, causing Alice to float out of her seat, her body only held in place by the safety harness. They hit tail first. Then the front wheels slammed down hard enough that twenty-thousand pounds of helicopter actually bounced back up by several feet, then they hit again and remained earthbound this time. The chopper rolled forward neatly across a handy ballpark's outfield.

"End simulation." Henderson remarked dryly.

"Roger end simulation." Emily acknowledged and in moments the rotors were biting air and they were once again aloft.

"Simulation?" Daniel shouted into the headset.

Emily Beale actually laughed. "Didn't want you to be able to say you'd ever flown with me without crashing."

"Crap!" was all Daniel offered.

Alice could feel him shaking with the post-adrenal fear-reaction. Okay, not one of her better jokes.

# # #

Daniel tried to beg off the repeat flight on the Mil Hound, but somehow Alice talked him into it. He'd been angry when he found out she was in on the joke, but Dr. Thompson proved to be a very difficult person to remain angry at.

Being angry was a skill Daniel had never developed. On purpose. He was often called unflappable and had always been proud that the petty sniping so traditional in D.C. politics didn't get to him. Not when clerking in the Senate, not when serving as the First Lady's personal secretary, and not when the Congressional Leadership was fighting him just for the sake of being pigheaded.

Alice managed to make it all her fault, though he knew Major Beale had played a significant role. But Alice was so upset that he'd agreed to make the second flight with minimal protest. He managed to keep his mouth shut and not say that he could think of little he'd like less while still on this side of the Apocalypse.

The Mi-4 Hound sounded completely different. The high whine of the Black Hawk's turbine engines was replaced by the buzz of the massive radial engine in the nose. The beat of the chopper blades wasn't all that different once they were underway. But despite the bigger cargo bay, Daniel felt quite claustrophobic.

On the Black Hawk, he'd been side-by-side with Alice. The open cargo doors had offered a wide view to the Virginian night and he hadn't felt any fear that he might fall, except for those few heart-stopping seconds of the emergency landing. He could observe the crew chiefs Big John and Crazy Tim sitting right in front of them and by looking up the middle, he'd been able to at least partly watch what the two pilots were doing.

On the Hound, he and Alice were seated across from each other on little fold-down metal seats amidships with only small, round porthole windows to offer any view. John and Tim actually lounged back on a pair of seats that were built into the rear doors that swung outward. With no miniguns and only one gauge on helicopter status, they had nothing to do during the flight. The cockpit was up a ladder and through a small hole, making the pilots almost unobservable.

And the front of his helmet didn't have an infrared view painted across the visor. It had clear plastic, so all he could see was the inside of the cabin.

The pilots weren't quiet on this ride.

"Let's run her an extra twenty feet high until we're sure of her," Henderson showing some caution.

His wife gave a running commentary, "Night vision has a lousy field of view low and forward. I don't dare try to terrain follow. Climbing an additional twenty."

Hard turns side-to-side threw Daniel back and forth between harness and hard metal hull of the chopper.

"She's tough, but she sure doesn't dance."

One of the crew chiefs chimed in with, "Don't ask us to shoot anything; we'd have to kick a hole in the side of the chopper and stick out a FN SCAR."

The Special Forces Combat Assault Rifle was very useful hand-to-hand, and each of the crew wore one across their chest as a matter of practice. Daniel felt far safer with the two mini-guns of the Black Hawk. Instead of the little rifle magazines that could fit in his hand, the miniguns fired thousands of rounds a minute from large boxes. He liked that.

Yes, it might be more clandestine to visit North Korea in a Mil Hound, but he'd take firepower when entering the most hostile country on the planet outside of Somalia.

This time they called "simulation" on the emergency landing test, but he didn't like it one bit more this time than the last.

They landed more slowly, but the helicopter complained much more loudly. Sheet metal banged as it flexed. The sharp ringing sound of the shock absorber right under his seat that sent him leaping against his harness made his ears hurt.

"Bottomed out the shocks there," one of the pilots remarked drily. "Not as forgiving as you'd expect."

Daniel was so wound up he couldn't even tell if it was Mark or Emily's voice. His leap was the only thing that had avoided a seriously bruised butt.

Moments after they were airborne, while they were still clawing for the altitude to clear the bleachers behind the baseball field, Beale shouted over the intercom.

"Incoming! Portside." An alarm sounded. "Cracked cylinder head, ten percent loss of power." Sure enough, the sound of the rotor blades slowed, faded ever so slightly.

The chopper veered to the right, away from the attack, but even Daniel could tell that it was sluggish.

Despite the deck heeling sharply, the two crew chiefs were on their feet. Their vests had a large D-ring on the front. Long tethers were snapped to them which let the chiefs move about the cabin. The other ends were clipped to metal loops in the ceiling.

Some visual signal passed between the two men. The giant one heaved open a side hatch close beside Daniel. The metal door slammed open so hard that the helicopter rang loudly enough to hurt Daniel's ears despite the protection of his helmet.

The shorter one, Tim Maloney, unslung his FN SCAR rifle and was aiming it out the door. Sergeant Big John Wallace held him in place with one fist wrapped around a handhold and the other grasping the back of Tim's flight vest.

There was no rattle of gunfire. No flash of— Tim's suit sounded an ear-piercing squeal!

"Shit!" Tim dropped to the floor still blocking part of the doorway.

Alice screamed and Daniel nearly did the same.

Big John crouched behind Tim and brought his own rifle to bear. Tim remained in place, apparently too wounded to move.

Without hesitation, Daniel reached across the middle of the helicopter's narrow cabin and pulled Alice's head down, as far toward his knees as the harness allowed, to reduce her exposure to incoming fire.

Daniel glanced back at the wounded crew chief even as he crouched over her. Tim's raised hand still grabbed the doorframe. He was wounded past being able to fight, but he was staying in place to act as a human shield for his fellow crew chief. Buying him precious moments to fend off the attackers. It was the bravest thing Daniel had ever seen.

That was when Daniel noticed the bright red flashes on the bulkhead right where Alice's head had been moments before.

Lasers. It was a training flight and they were being shot with lasers. Tim's suit must have registered him as hit in the firefight. That's why it had squealed, a hit. And why his rifle, and now John's, sounded with no rattle of gunfire.

It was only a mock battle.

Despite that, Daniel was still impressed that Tim had shielded his friend with his own body. He couldn't imagine doing such a thing. To want to protect someone so much that your instinct put you in front of the bullets.

Once they were in the clear, Daniel realized that he still had Alice trapped down across his knees. Even if he couldn't imagine throwing himself in front of the bullet, his instincts apparently had other ideas about who he wanted to protect.

Chapter 17

"You have the strangest idea of what constitutes a date." Daniel's smile was soft and his voice teasing. He'd walked Alice to her apartment door and now they huddled under the narrow porch roof to escape from the light snow that started falling as Daniel drove her home.

Alice admitted she'd bit off more than she'd intended. Her nerves were still freaking out. The attack had seemed so real, her death so imminent. Nothing in the CIA's S.A.D. training had prepared her for the reality of SOAR training. Of course, all they'd gotten from S.A.D. as non-combatants was a helicopter ride and a quick thirty-minute flight in a jet that could flip and roll better than any amusement park ride.

What she hadn't been prepared for was the realism. Or that Daniel had thrown himself between Alice and the attackers, simulated or not. She'd always stood up for herself, known she was on her own.

He ran a gentle thumb over her lower lip, his fingertips brushing her cheek, cradling it with a tenderness that brought tears to her eyes and a pounding to her heart that she'd only read of and scoffed at in books.

She wanted to run inside and weep at the wonder of a man who would willing sacrifice his life for hers, even in simulation. She wanted a cup of hot cocoa with a very large shot of brandy in it to calm the jitters. And Alice also wanted to drag Daniel into bed and lose herself in the throes of the passion that was raging for release. A passion she'd kept safely under wraps her whole life because no one had ever called it forth.

Alice slid her hand up Daniel's chest and around his neck. She pulled him down to her, their breath steamy in the cold night air mingling, merging, and gone when their lips met.

A warmth spread through her as he tipped her back the last few inches until she lay back against her own closed front door. The soft porch light shone down over Daniel, lighting him like an angel. Her own personal angel.

She couldn't stop the smile crossing her lips.

Daniel smiled back in response and pulled back just far enough to speak. "What?"

"Sounds stupid." And it did.

"Say it anyway."

She looked up into his eyes and over his shoulder saw a Secret Service agent standing just a few paces back.

"I'm sorry, sir, but you've been called back to the White House." He held out a cell phone.

In moments, with barely a word beyond "South Africa conference again," a few choice moments of silence when any less tactful man would curse a blue streak, and a final light brush of fingertips down her cheek in apology, Alice lay alone against her front door and Daniel was giving rapid instructions over the phone as they hustled him back to the escort car.

She unlocked the doors and turned on the hallway light. As usual, the mess that was her apartment had not magically rectified itself during her absence.

"Is that the kind of life you want?" Alice asked the empty room. The lack of privacy. The inability to complete something you hadn't even started yet.

She didn't know which was more shocking, that she even considered asking the question or that the answer was yes. For this man, it just might be worth it.

Chapter 18

Daniel listened to the phone ring in his ear while ignoring the pile on his desk. It had actually lowered over the last week, just not as much as it needed to.

All week Daniel had fought against two conflicting agendas: the tide on his desk and finding a moment to actually see Alice. To discover what might lay past those kisses of hers that were so much richer than the best apple cider fresh off the press. Through the calendar's nightly treats of a candy on an elastic bracelet to a tiny chocolate bar and a half dozen other variations, he'd only managed to spend time with Dr. Alice Thompson on the phone.

He'd seen Henderson twice and Beale three times as they continued testing the possible scenarios for infiltrating a heavily militarized, paranoid country not once but twice two days apart.

But not Alice.

It was really quite unsatisfying in so many ways. But she'd made it clear that no matter what time he called, she'd gladly answer the phone. It might take a few minutes before her words were actually comprehensible, but once she was awake, they talked easily and often long.

Still no answer. Usually she'd answer by now.

Yet it didn't feel real or satisfying. Maybe the whole thing was in his head. Maybe she was merely being nice on the phone. He could feel a distance building. A couple of premature kisses and a pair of heart-stopping helicopter flights didn't make up for a week apart.

And when they talked, he felt... They talked far more about him than her. She was the one he wanted to know about. Instead, they talked about the family farm in Tennessee.

How he'd come to Washington to promote the Slow Food movement in the southeast. She didn't know about that and they'd spent whole conversations discussing seasonal and local rather than unsustainable farming and having to ship food immense distances. To eat the flour that was made from the wheat just down the road, Daniel's research had shown that the nearest flour mill was five hundred miles away. His local wheat had to travel a thousand miles just to become flour, never mind be baked.

He reluctantly reached out to cut the connection. He hung onto the receiver, considering calling her cell phone. But it was nearly midnight. Maybe he should just leave her be. He didn't want to speak to her on the phone anyway. He wanted to hold her close. He wanted his world to stop the way it did when she rested her head on his shoulder. He wanted to know about her.

When he did manage to turn the conversation to being about her, it was her professional life they explored. Her work was truly fascinating to him.

He'd always been a people person, almost as good a negotiator and peacemaker as the President. The President excelled on the larger issues; averting national strikes, international relations, and so on. Daniel's specialty was becoming the fine art of convincing the swing vote on a key bill. They'd recently passed a very controversial education financing package and Daniel had stood at the center of it. It had been his victory.

And once again, Dr. Alice Thompson would somehow not be the topic of conversation. Maybe if he had the FBI pull a file on her he'd find out something. Surely the FBI would have a file on a senior CIA analyst. Wouldn't they?

Daniel set the phone back in the cradle and stared out his office window. The ledge was the perfect height to prop his feet and stare past the tips of his polished shoes. Something he'd never done until Alice had propped her green and red sneakers on his desk almost two weeks ago. Beyond the heavy glass, the White House grounds spread before him, brightly lit as always. That was one thing that the movies got wrong, it was never dark inside the White House without closing heavy curtains.

He knew he shouldn't turn around, his desk would just be there waiting for him. He had to get focused on the North Korea problem, but the ever-shifting files and crises kept it off the top of his list.

A clandestine visit could be anything from a defection to personal bribery in exchange for vague promises to stop their next space launch. That the latest launch had shredded itself shortly after liftoff and scattered debris over the Yellow Sea hadn't mitigated the serious international furor.

Alice had said something in their conversation yesterday. She didn't speak much during their phone calls and Daniel often lost the thread of their conversations when she did speak. Her voice was calm and soothing, and he had to admit sometimes he simply enjoyed listening to the lilt and flow.

He couldn't pin down her accent at all. A D.C. resident who didn't have that soft touch of the South. But neither did she have the New York rhythms, though she did admit to being raised there in addition to schooling there.

It was a voice he could listen to for hours... But she didn't speak on the phone.

That was it. So much of Daniel's life was done by phone. Calls to the Hill, overseas with the assistants of other world leaders, that was his comfort zone. Alice, so open and cheerful in person, was, at best, reticent on the phone.

He dropped his feet to the floor and stared out at the white oak tree beyond his window. Bare of leaves it spread its arms in reaching majesty. It had been too long since he'd been out in the country. Camp David a couple of times, but he hadn't been down to visit his dad or sister on the farm in at least six months, maybe closer to a year. If they hadn't come to D.C. every month or so for a visit he'd have gone crazy from missing them.

That's what he had to do. He had to get out of the White House and go see Dr. Alice Thompson. See if there was more behind those few kisses that turned his well-ordered mind into a cloud of confetti. She didn't mind whatever hour he called, maybe she'd be okay if he just showed up instead.

Without turning from the window, he reached back for his phone. He punched for the Secret Service office.

"Hi, I'd like a car." He told the on-duty officer who answered. "Destination is Woodmont, the home of Dr. Thompson."

He hung up the phone, nodded to himself in the window. Good decision. Do something for Daniel rather than the country. He liked the way that felt. It felt right.

A gift. He should bring her a gift. Especially since he'd be rousting her out of bed.

There was a thought to stop him. Daniel found it very easy to imagine how Dr. Thompson would look tousled with sleep, blinking up at him through a partially open front door.

He spun back to his desk seeking something better than a White House-logoed mug and there she was. Sitting in his chair as if she'd been there a while.

Daniel searched for words. Found none.

He blinked twice. Still there. A third time. No change.

Her smile grew, "You might want to raise your jaw. It looks funny all open like that."

He managed to close it.

"You're here?" It came out as little more than a croak.

She reached out with one of those beautiful, slim-fingered hands and poked a single finger against her thigh as if testing.

"Yes, I appear to actually be here."

"That's why you didn't answer your phone."

She nodded.

"You were here when I called you."

"I could hear the ring. Something like fourteen times. How deaf do you think I am?"

Daniel didn't know what to do with that one and decided the wisest course might be to just let it go.

"I did like that you'd memorized my number rather than just setting me up on speed dial."

Then he'd avoid mentioning that he barely knew how to work the new phone system. And hers was the only number he'd called during his year in this office that wasn't routed through Janet.

"You are going to say something substantive eventually, aren't you?"

He nodded but still couldn't find the clutch to engage his brain.

Her laugh rippled out and up, rising a quick octave.

That finally shook him loose. He rose and circled the desk, or started to.

His jacket caught the stack of files on the desk and only a quick dive saved a repeat performance of the earlier night. By the time he had the mess stabilized and dared once more turn his attention on Alice, she too had risen to her feet.

"I—"

She raised a hand, palm out. "Nothing mundane."

That threw out the half dozen sentences that tumbled into his mind. "I'm so glad to see you. Why are you here? How…" Nope. Chuck them all.

Daniel could converse with world leaders, charm their children, placate their wives. Why couldn't he be coherent around Dr. Alice Thompson.

He considered, then edged slightly away from the desk and its teetering paperwork.

Alice tilted her head sideways as if listening to the late night silence of the West Wing.

No sound. More importantly no light from the open door leading to the Oval Office. If Daniel could take time to do one thing, it would be what had been in the forefront of his thoughts since the last time he'd been with her.

He leaned in to kiss those smiling lips. Raised a hand to brush back her hair so that he'd be able to watch both of her eyes close on a sigh. And—his phone buzzed.

He cursed. "No!" He growled at Alice from a mere inch away. "Let the world run on its own for one blasted moment."

"The car." Alice told him as the phone buzzed again.

"What car?"

"The one you ordered."

"I ordered a car?" All he could concentrate on at the moment was that Alice was here. So close he could feel the warmth of her skin on his cheeks. The phone's shrill buzz was not helping the moment.

"To come see me. There was some reason you wanted to see me. What was that?"

The phone interrupted his response. He answered it with what he could only describe as a snarl.

"Your car is ready, sir."

"Why would I want a car?"

The agent sputtered for a moment.

Alice rested a hand on the center of his chest, toying a little with his tie where it stuck up out of the vest. She tugged him down by it until her lips were by his open ear.

"So that we can neck like teenagers in the backseat." Her breathy whisper tickled.

"Uh," he managed. That was almost exactly why he'd wanted a car. He'd had some idea of talking with Dr. Alice Thompson face to face, perhaps over a glass of wine and getting to know her. But he'd also had a clear idea of that slumberous look he'd imagined.

"I," he cleared his throat twice before he could continue, "uh, won't be needing it after all. Thanks." He did his best to get the phone back in the cradle but knew he fumbled it badly.

He turned back to kiss her. But it was too much, too fast. No matter how much he wanted her, it was a lousy way to run a relationship. An even worse way to start one.

"I," was all he managed.

Her smile had shifted, subtley, from amused to soft. "It seems you missed me."

He nodded. Not trusting to words yet.

She glanced up at him through those bangs.

This time, his hand rose more naturally to brush her curls aside. He cupped her cheek and leaned into a kiss.

They moaned in unison.

Daniel couldn't pull her close enough.

He didn't have the strength to take her home.

He didn't have the patience to take Alice upstairs.

Daniel broke the kiss and walked away.

Chapter 19

Alice stumbled a half step forward as Daniel strode away from her across his office.

This couldn't be happening.

For a week his voice had filled her ears, her thoughts, and was now invading her dreams. His stories of his life had wrapped around her until she could taste them more clearly than his first kiss.

It had taken all of her bravery to come to him, to find her way back to the office of the White House Chief of Staff. To expose herself to whatever Daniel's reaction might be.

She watched him close a door to his secretary's office.

Yet Daniel had never explained his reactions during the conversation at the piano in any of those late night phone calls. He'd never said why he had turned from her and practically run from the room at that dinner with President. The man radiated such light, but some darkness tore at him. It tore at her too, like a knife.

He closed the door to the hallway.

Alice steadied herself with a hand on the edge of Daniel's desk. She'd come to the White House because there was no one else she could trust to test an idea she'd had about North Korea. An idea too impossible to trust, yet it ate at her until it reaching the tipping point between skepticism and possibility.

His reaction to her had been electric. Listening to his frustration of trying to call her had been funny and absolutely charming.

Daniel closed the door to the Oval Office. Then he leaned his forehead against it. As if wrestling with something. How to tell her they were done? That couldn't be it.

Maybe she'd ruined it by coming here. On the phone, fine, but not in person. No one who knew her wanted her. All too intimidated that they weren't the smartest in the room. All those men who couldn't handle how easily she saw through their games and stratagems.

Daniel was the first man she couldn't read. She'd thought there was something there, but she'd been wrong.

She pulled up her shields and turned to run from the room.

Daniel hadn't moved. He still leaned against the door. Then actually turned a key, an old brass key, in the door to the Oval Office.

Alice could hear the bolt click home in the echoing silence of the room. Then Daniel turned to look at her, his back against the door he'd just bolted.

She'd misjudged? Could his need for her possibly match her own for him? Her mother's voice was asking how could she use this to her own gain, and Alice did her best to shove that aside.

Alice's own question dragged her across the dark green oriental carpet that covered most of the dark wood floor.

He watched her without moving. His eyes a dark blue so intense that no shield could stop his gaze. She'd worn a knit red sweater, intricate with clockwork cables that she'd had to tear out a half-dozen times in order to make them right.

Not once as she approached did he look down at her sweater. Not at her chest. Not at her jean-wrapped hips. Not at her sneakers, red with green laces this time. All he did was watch her eyes, and she couldn't look away. If there'd been a chair or table between them, she'd have walked square into it.

Only when she came to a halt did he react.

He reached a hand as if to tentatively stroke her from shoulder to elbow, but let it brush air instead, then drop to his side.

Alice watched him a moment longer. Trying desperately to read his face.

For half a moment she considered calling his bluff. Perhaps toss off some funny line.

It was a half moment too long.

Daniel swept her into his arms. He'd have knocked the wind from her lungs if his mouth had not already covered hers. She wrapped her arms around his neck so that there was no possibility of him walking away from her this time.

The fire of need wrapped around them despite the chill December night beyond the window. She'd never been the forward one in sex, but she had his tie pulled loose and his vest and shirt undone so that she could curl against his chest. It was as beautiful as when he'd been pumping iron over in the residence. That she'd been prepared for.

What took her totally unawares was the softness of his skin and the heat of it. This was a place dreams were born.

With a near shoulder-dislocating wrench, he shed his coat vest and shirt into a pile on the floor. She wrapped herself next to his warmth like a good winter blanket. It was only half a surprise that they were skin to skin. She hadn't noticed the loss of her sweater and ever-present turtleneck.

"Wow! Dr. Thompson." He was holding her out at half arm's length and looking down at her torso.

She went to cover herself with her arms. "What?"

"First, you need to know that I have an excellent imagination."

"So?" She got one arm free and across her chest.

With the gentlest motion he took her wrist and moved her arm out of the way.

She'd never felt so naked in her life.

"I never imagined how good you could look. Not even in that knock-out evening gown. You're beautiful."

The heat flashed to her face. Cute? Sure, she'd been called that. But beautiful? Not that she could recall. Not ever.

He was smiling down at her.

"What!?" It came out with more force than she'd intended.

"You're blush starts lower than I expected."

She glanced down at the fair skin atop her breasts, the capillaries now flushed with blood attempting to release the heat coursing through her.

Some rebellious part of her self-defense mechanisms rose to the fore. "Well, what are you going to do about it?"

His smile grew. Grew until it lit his eyes. Damn! She could almost swear they twinkled. Why not? Christmas was coming after all.

"I'll revel!" And with that he leaned down and did just that.

Chapter 20

Alice stretched comfortably back to consciousness.

No surprise revelation of where they'd landed. Daniel's bedroom. Daniel's bed. A sturdy four-poster that had belonged to an 1800s President. He'd said he liked the bed. So had she. It was a beautiful piece of furniture, and if she'd had a couple of bathrobe belts handy, she might have tied him to it. She'd have blushed at the thought, if he hadn't suggested doing the same to her.

In Daniel's office, with no protection handy, they'd still done more on his office carpet than two kids ever did in any backseat. At some point they'd dressed, traversed the corridors, and used the elevator to the third floor so that they wouldn't disturb the President on the second floor.

Alice did her best to not look at the Secret Service agents they'd passed in the lower halls. Even if the agents didn't reveal knowing looks, she knew they were there, carefully masked by neutral expressions.

Some of them did smile at her as she gawked at the decorations. Even the lower level passage of the Center Hall had been strewn.

"Last year was pretty somber, so recently after the First Lady's death," Daniel had told her. "I think we're overcompensating this year, but it is terribly cheerful."

She couldn't argue on either point. The length of half a football field, it had been done as a Christmas in miniature. Walls had been lined with multi-tiered villages, as if the Swiss Alps had been shrunk down to fit into the White House. You could spend a week and never see it all.

She smiled to herself, remembering they'd spent less than five minutes in their desperate need to get upstairs.

Here Daniel did have protection and they'd made use of it until they were so exhausted and sweaty that they'd scampered down the hall wearing only a couple of his dress shirts, through the Music Room, and up the half-flight of stairs to stand on the wintery Promenade. They'd had to dance foot-to-foot because the deck glittered with a dusting of frozen dew. They'd held each other so close that they were almost warm enough despite the freezing temperature as they watched the chill moonlight battle the nighttime lights of D.C.

They'd scrambled back inside, plunged into a hot shower and fallen back into bed.

Yes, she knew exactly where she'd woken. No surprise there.

Where she'd woken alone. Also not a real shocker. It was mid-morning by the discrete bedside clock and Daniel would have plunged into meetings long since.

The surprise instead was how she felt.

Her body was languid and supple after such an incredible bout. Sore in more than a few spots, but Daniel was a gentle lover, even at his most energetic. Despite her fair skin, she didn't see a single mark. Alice wasn't sure if her body had ever felt this good.

But that bone-deep made-of-liquid feeling didn't surprise her either. It was the guilt. She felt no guilt about the sex, they'd both enjoyed it far too much for that.

No, Alice felt bothered by her own silence. Daniel had again probed into her past. Ever so gently, in that immensely tactful way she'd learned was the trademark of a very successful man. But she could feel his disappointment as she again evaded describing a past she'd much rather disown. He no longer fell for her redirection and razzle dazzle subject changes. He wanted to know about her past. Didn't he understand how little it had to do with her present?

She dragged her lazy bones out of bed. There was a probably a maid waiting somewhere, but she did her best to reorganize the royal blue flannel sheets and the Irish Double-Chain quilt done in rich cheery golds and Kelly greens. She rubbed her fingers over it. Hand-stitched and a really fine job of it. Maybe from his family farm. She liked to think of that being his touch of home.

The rest of the room radiated maleness, with rich walnut wainscoting and white-on-white patterned wallpaper. A massive dresser stood staunchly in the corner, matched in style to the sturdy bed. The top was decorated with just two photos. She eased over and inspected them.

First, clearly a family photo. They were an impressive group. Daniel stood out for his beauty, but his sister could do very well in a pageant herself. The photo had captured Mom, Dad, gold retriever, and a big blue tractor the same color Daniel's eyes had been last night. They had shone with a brilliance the moment before he jumped her. Or had she jumped him first?

Second, was a close-up of the sister. Her look was wicked. Just her shoulders and head showing above water that must be in a flowing stream. It was apparent that she had no swimsuit and was not in the least amused by her brother's camera. The look promised a painful retribution. Alice could feel herself smiling at recognizing the shared moment, even if she didn't know the whole story.

She'd have to ask.

Which brought her back to the guilt that kept tickling up her spine. Daniel would tell her anything, and she'd tell him nothing. It was an unfair bargain and she didn't know what to do about it. Alice didn't want to destroy what they had.

She turned for the shower, going past the red leather armchair that held her neatly folded clothes, including the sweater she'd lost somewhere in the hallway. Maybe it had been during their brief stop at the grand piano. No, they'd made love beneath that shortly before getting a late night snack in the kitchen. Early morning snack. The sweater had been long since gone by then.

She stood under the hot shower spray, appreciating the pressure that could deliver a needling massage even here at the top of the building.

The problem was during those moments they'd curled together to briefly recover. Her head on his shoulder, her hand tracing the fine outlines of his chest. Or when he'd curled against her, one ear resting in the center of her breastbone as he listened to her heart.

He'd left her silences to speak into, and she hadn't. She'd felt them grow and expand, take on shape in the dark of the heavily curtained bedroom.

Alice notched up the heat in the shower a bit more, she'd always favored a searing hot shower.

She knew what he wanted. He'd made it clear in the last few phone calls as well. No matter how intimate they were, she was terrified of destroying it by bringing up her past. To someone like Daniel, the past was everything. Filled with family and life and joy. Poster boy for a good upbringing.

While her past hadn't had the terror that some of her friends had, it was just not something that existed anymore. She'd discarded it all and rebuilt herself in her own image. She even had an imagined past; one she shared only reluctantly so that people didn't probe. But with Daniel, each time she tried to pull out the granny who'd raised her after her dad had left and her mother died... It was just wrong. She hadn't been able to lie to him.

What did it matter that she didn't have a past? She was Dr. Alice Thompson, self-made woman.

She rinsed her hair and did her best to pretend that all of the water running down her cheeks came out of the showerhead.

Chapter 21

"You dog."

Daniel just laughed which only increased the President's smile. They sat across from each other in the West Wing presidential dining room. The European Union's latest Greece-bailout plan covered the parts of the table that weren't already covered with sausage, pepper, and onion sandwiches, macaroni salad, and potato chips. Tall glasses of iced tea perched on cork coasters.

"You finally saw her."

Daniel nodded. Did way more than see her. He did his best to hide his smile in a large bite of crunchy hoagie roll. Knew he'd been too slow by Peter Matthews' smile.

"Good?"

There were a dozen layers to the question.

"Really good. The sandwich that is," he spoke around a partially chewed bite, but wasn't fooling Peter in the slightest.

"Good." This time the statement was definitive. The President's approval a tangible thing of great importance.

"I think we did way better than 'Really good.'" A woman's voice sounded from the doorway. "'Great!' would at least get you in the right ballpark."

Daniel stumbled to his feet and attempted to swallow nearly choking himself. Alice stood in the doorway to the dining room. She radiated. There was no other word for it. She slouched lightly against a doorframe and looked at perfect ease. Her hair, still slightly damp in spots she'd missed with the blow dryer, a shining cloud about her face. Her eyes were wicked.

The President rose much more elegantly and crossed to her. He took her hand, and shook it with that perfect, real sincerity that Peter Matthews brought to everything he did.

"Good afternoon, Dr. Thompson. Care to join us for lunch?"

She nodded her assent and crossed to the table.

Daniel shoved some of the Greece plan toward the other end of the table, and one of the ushers had a place set even before the President had tucked her chair in beneath her.

"If you don't kiss her good morning, I will."

Daniel finished his swallow, wiped his mouth with a napkin, and did just that. Reveled for just a moment in how soft her lips were. Knew enough about her now to feel both the bright smile and the nervousness beneath. He squeezed her hand in encouragement, a gesture quickly returned, before he returned to his seat.

"We were just taking a quick look at the EU bailout plan for Greece. They dropped twenty billion Euro, twenty-five billion dollars, and it appears to finally be working six months later."

"Now if only the same thing could work in a U.S. market, Mr. President." Alice offered brightly as someone set a plate and sandwich down in front of her.

The President sighed. "The previous administration dropped half a trillion dollars, and mostly it shuffled the balance of problems around. Mitigated the worst of the disasters, but we're still a long way from a solution."

Daniel offered the President a nod. The President had known that Alice would be nervous and chosen a neutral topic to allow her a moment to land. Walking in on the middle of being the subject of conversation... Not good. Really not good.

And the President continued until Daniel found himself able to enter the conversation as well. For twenty minutes or more, they explored general topics while simultaneoulsy working their way through the lunch spread before them.

After they'd set plates aside, and the ushers had swept them away, he could see Alice clearly had something on her mind.

He nodded to her and she smiled back at the encouragement.

"I actually came to see you last night for a, ah, another reason."

#

Alice took a deep breath, thankful that at least the President showed a steady hand. No wry glance at Daniel. No roll of his eyes.

Daniel, on the other hand, should never get near a poker table. He had progressed through a dozen shades of red and twice as many stages of awkwardness since she had invited herself to lunch.

"Good." Somehow, there'd been a whole conversation between them, all wrapped up in one, single word. Guy speak was so strange. Maybe that's why her father had never spoken. Could never even get his one word in edgewise past his wife.

Clear your head, Alice. Back to business.

"I have a theory. And it's a little on the completely whacked-out side of possibility."

The two men nodded in unison, sharing a neat sense of accord. The President waved the ushers out, and the door behind Alice closed with a discrete click.

"I presume we're discussing North Korea."

She nodded to the President. Right. These two could talk about twenty different countries a day. She, however, was only paid to care about one at the moment.

"Who are you planning to send to the meeting?" She'd decided to cast aside any lingering doubts about whether or not there would actually be a meeting. It had been someone else's task to determine the efficacy of that original request. Her task was to decide what to do about it if it was real.

The problem was the backcheck to verify the situation, however in the world that was done. The response hadn't come through the same channel. The first had been a simply encrypted message, just sufficient to stop prying eyes, but not requiring the NSA to crack it either. The message had passed off to an NGO. Some Non-Governmental Organization that had been granted a three-day pass into North Korea to test for mercury in the coastal waters. They'd come out with a message in hand.

"Daniel has suggested Vincent, the deputy ambassador to the U.N. I was more inclined to Elisa, the Assistant Secretary of State. We never got much past that. Why?"

Alice sipped at her iced tea to buy a moment to collate factors, but they didn't change. The backcheck had come from the conductor of the Sea of Blood Opera Company at a carefully staged performance in Paris. An abruptly scheduled event, very reminiscent of the 1972 North Korean circus ensemble who had stormed Paris the week before Nixon went to China.

"We could send somebody military, that is if you think that's more appropriate." Daniel's idea.

"I believe," Alice rolled her mental dice and came up double-sixes. A good backgammon roll; the same one that had landed her in Daniel's bed last night. Which had been amazingly worth it. What the hell! Play the game! Double or nothing.

"I believe that we're thinking too small. I think that the Vice President is the minimum you should send, but that you Mr. President should be prepared to follow immediately if not attend yourself."

The President started to shake his head, then noticed Daniel's silence.

Alice studied Daniel as well. In the last few seconds he'd done that mercurial shift; this time from slightly fumbling lover to most astute advisor to the most powerful man on the planet.

She could see the cogs turning. Shifting the pieces to include what he knew of the situation, and what he knew of her.

"What don't I know?" his question came after a full thirty seconds of echoing silence.

"Methods of communication of the two messages. Personalities of the individuals who I termed the Top Six, the highest advisors and leaders in the North Korean regime."

"The personalities I know; which is why I had difficulty accepting your initial report. Two messages?"

"Original channel and backcheck."

"Which were?"

She shook her head. Alice wasn't even supposed to know, but Director Smith had released the data to her when she'd insisted it was necessary to assess the request's authenticity. Names and exact movements had been expunged from the reports she read, but there was no questioning them. However, she also wasn't at any liberty to reveal them, not even to the President.

Again that silence. Daniel stood and walked slowly to the window and back. God! The man even moved beautifully. She could spend a day simply watching him walk about, with or without clothes.

And in addition to beauty, she realized his other blazingly attractive quality to her; Daniel Drake Darlington would have made an amazing analyst. She could she him working through the possibilities. Interpreting and discarding them far faster than she had. Of course she'd had to build up from a blank slate. He'd had a head start built by her reports and information. Still he—

A low whistle indicated that he'd reached the same conclusion she had. He shook his head in clear rejection of his own conclusions being too preposterous. Definitely the same result she'd synthesized in eight days of hard work.

But finally he turned to her and softly voiced a question, "Really?"

She nodded, which appeared to cut his knees out from under him and dropped him back into his chair.

The President turned from one to the other and finally said, "No. That's not possible." But drew it out in a tone revealing he too would have made a fine analyst.

Chapter 22

"I can't believe that you talked me into this!" Daniel had to shout above the roar of the C-17's jet engines and the air being plowed aside at five hundred miles an hour. The Black Hawk helicopter crew were up at the front of the plane. He and Alice sat about halfway down the side of the immense cargo plane.

Alice didn't deign to answer. If her conclusion was right, and the Supreme Leader of North Korea was the one requesting the conference with the American government, then the President had to be ready to appear on a moment's notice.

Daniel's afternoon had been immediately hijacked from all other considerations. Added to that, a second sleepless night in a row, planning and coordinating this time, left him feeling lightheaded and hazy.

Now he was flying West to verify a portion of the preparation personally.

"What did Janet give you in the calendar tonight?" Alice sat on the next fold-down seat mounted along the side of the plane. They were hard and his butt hurt.

The woman was going to make him crazy. He checked his watch. Three in the afternoon. Fourteen hours ago he'd been having a nice sit down lunch with the President, now he was freezing his behind at thirty-thousand feet. How had this happened?

"The sun hasn't even come up yet." Especially not the mid-winter D.C. sun. "And we're flying West through the time zones. We won't even land until sunrise never mind sunset. Now you want to break your own rules?"

They sat in heavy parkas on barely padded seats. They should have pulled on the flightsuits when they were offered, but he'd thought a ski parka would be sufficient. They kept the air inside the plane heated, but the metal skin of the hull sucked the heat right out of his bones.

Two Black Hawk helicopters were aboard. Their rotors had been folded over their tails and they'd been slid in tail-to-tail. The Mil Hound was nowhere to be seen and the two Black Hawks looked absolutely vicious. These were attack craft, weapons hanging to either side from stub wings. Missiles, machine guns, something they'd told him was a cannon able to fire rounds wider than his thumb at a rate over eighty times per second. He'd assumed Major Henderson was kidding, but maybe not. He didn't seem the type to joke about weaponry.

Alice grabbed his arm and rolled his wrist toward her so that she could see the watch upside down.

"Looks like nine-thirty to me. You know, you should get a watch that has those little numbers instead of just hashy marks. It would help you read time better."

"Another of your mother's rules? Adjust everything around you to suit yourself?"

Some of the light went out of Alice's eyes and she released his wrist. She drifted off to a silent place. A place he suddenly feared because maybe he couldn't reach her when she went there.

He did the only thing he could think of and pulled the Advent Calendar book out of his flight bag.

"Now let's see." He turned it so that she could look at it with him. Her face aimed down and her bangs flopped over her eyes, he hoped she was looking with him.

He did his best to make it a cozy moment, despite the need to shout to be heard above the engines.

"I seem of have eaten the first page out of house and home." He made a show of inspecting inside each of the eight pull tab windows on the first page. Sure enough, all empty. He'd described each to her on the phone, but now she could see them one by one. And they were lovely art work.

He turned to the middle page.

This image was a grand sweep of delicate art. A sleigh piled with gifts and a dozen tiny micedeer perched on a roof peak as if they did it every day. Daniel had already eaten the caramel behind the door showing where Santa's hat had caught on a brick inside the chimney.

Around the Christmas tree, a balding but undeniably jolly Saint Hamster, in a red and white jumpsuit that barely contained his furry girth, was scattering presents from his bag.

Daniel opened day ten; a tiny drawing of milk and cookies half eaten, the nibble distinctly two-toothed. Day eleven; inside, a naughty kitten trying to peek through a child-gate pulled across the head of the stairs. Day twelve, behind a picture of great uncle Rex; the good kitten asleep in bed. Day thirteen, Daniel could finally feel Alice's smile though he couldn't see it, a tiny mouse behind a tiny mouse hole curled up and fast asleep in a nest of red-and-green wrapping paper.

Day fourteen; the fourteenth of December, was a tall door running right up the length of the tree's trunk. Inside were a pair of tiny candy canes, shorter than his pinky. Somehow Janet once again knew there would be two of them together. And once again, he'd missed the addition to the calendar's pages.

Two weeks. He'd only known Alice two weeks. It was unimaginable. Partly because he'd had sex with her, he'd never done that so soon, and also because he couldn't imagine a day when he couldn't at least speak with her. How had she become so important so quickly?

Daniel handed one of the candy canes to Alice and took the other himself. As they peeled off the plastic, they looked inside the calendar window to see a different version of the tree. Smaller, standing still in the woods with its companion trees. Somehow it looked to be asleep wearing a little nightcap of snow, and it had a dream bubble reaching up into a starry sky of being a real Christmas tree someday when it grew up.

"So, do you taste like a candy cane?" When Daniel brushed her cheek, she looked up at him with a slow reluctance. He didn't say anything. Didn't ask anything. He simply kissed her. Long and slow and deep, reveling in the taste of her. The feel of her.

He pulled back just a little and nodded. "Yep! Alice and candy cane. Knew that was a winner combination without even guessing."

Her smile thanked him for not pushing. The eyes, those amazing hazeled eyes, he wished he could borrow a bit of elf magic and wipe them clear of whatever bad memory still lurked there. She held his hand tightly in hers, and leaned her head on his shoulder.

Daniel leaned back against the hull of the aircraft, feeling the vibration become a part of his body. With the Advent Calendar across his lap in one hand, and Alice's fingers wrapped warmly in his other hand, Daniel could feel content. As if he were in the right place at the right time.

He rested his cheek on Alice's impossibly soft hair, closed his eyes, and let the exhaustion of a pair of sleepless nights take him under.

Chapter 23

Daniel tried to assess him, but the man was so totally non-descript that Daniel never would have noticed him on the street. Now they sat in a small restaurant at Skagit County airport, which sat in a far corner of Washington State.

"Captain Smith," the man they'd flown across the country to meet smiled with a bit of chagrin, "My real name, I promise."

Captain Smith of the Canadian Special Operations Aviation Squadron. SOAS was one of those special forces groups that almost no one had heard of. They weren't Delta or SEAL or SAS, but they were impressively effective in their own quiet way. Daniel had read the reports carefully when Beale had recommended he contact them.

He and Alice, Majors Beale and Henderson, and Captain Smith sat upstairs in the restaurant looking out over parked private planes and the sleepy runways. At the far end of the room, a half dozen vacant tables scattered across the space between them, sat the two Black Hawk crew chiefs, Tim and John.

No one else. The waitress had returned downstairs to fill their various breakfast orders.

Almost lost in the rainy haze, dull gray against the gray-green of the moss-covered fir trees, the C-17 transport lurked on an unused taxiway at the back of the airport. The flight crew had remained there as a standing guard. The flight engineer was downstairs getting some breakfasts to go for them.

No scheduled flights bounced through Skagit, not until the tulip season. The waitress, recognizing them as obvious out-of-towners, had regaled them with stories about the local farms which supplied ninety percent of the nation's tulips. The wall was hung with dozens of colorful photos offering mute testament to her statements about the number of sight-seeing flights in the high season. Each incongruously draped with red-and-green Christmas garlands that had seen a few too many seasons.

The two crew chiefs were sitting nonchalantly by the head of the stairs at the opposite end of their otherwise vacant dining area. Big John, the giant of the pair, was riffling a deck of cards. Tim, "Crazy Tim" Daniel had been informed, had tossed some coins on the table. Daniel had learned enough about them to know that no matter how casual they appeared, they were intently watching the parking lot out the window, listening for stray noises from the main restaurant below, and guarding each other's back. They moved with that perfect harmony of good friends and immense training.

"Skagit County airport in mid-December," Captain Smith observed. "Stone quiet and perhaps a twenty-minute flight for the U.S.-Canadian border. I find those are interesting aspects of your curious locale for a meeting."

"Captain Nathaniel Smith?" Alice asked with surprise, emphasizing the first name.

He nodded easily.

"You flew the Sudanese mission in 2006?"

The man didn't move. He'd shifted from a pleasant man with a light British accent to cold steel in a single heartbeat.

The crew chiefs sensing the change visibly tensed at the far end of the room. The majors set down their coffee cups ever so nonchalantly, probably to empty their hands in case sudden action was required.

Daniel braced to interpose himself between the man and Alice. Captain Smith would be easy to remember now. The captain, so common-looking a moment ago, now radiated the chill of death.

"That was well done, sir." Alice held out her hand. "I'd be honored to shake your hand."

Captain Smith gingerly shook her hand as if she were a grenade about to go off in his grasp.

Daniel recognized the look, as if the Captain's brain had just been sideswiped by a speeding locomotive. Daniel often felt that way around Alice.

The two Majors inspected the Captain more carefully, but Daniel could see by their quick exchange of looks that neither knew what Alice was referring to. He didn't either.

"How?" the Captain's voice was rough.

"That was approximately the same time that I was performing a departmental assessment of flight abilities of various allied Special Forces operators. Your career has been, I believe 'distinguished' would be a fitting word. Naturally when I learned that the asset of a close U.S. ally had flown the mission, there was a eighty-five percent probability you had been on that flight."

"Uh, I was commander of the mission."

"Seventy-two percent probability. Yes!" Alice raised her hand palm out and the Captain high-fived her before he could stop himself.

Captain Smith glanced around the table, eyed each of them warily before returning his attention to Alice. He rubbed his fingers together as if the high-five had somehow changed their texture.

"What are you?"

Daniel leaned forward, ready to jump to her defense, but she simply offered one of those disarming smiles.

"I'm a specialist in logistics. There are perhaps a dozen people in the world who could recognize your trademark actions, if they bothered to look, maybe only a half dozen. I'm one of them."

Once again he assessed the circle about the table, then offered a soft laugh.

"My job is to be invisible. I find it, ah, less than reassuring that I am not."

Alice patted his arm. "If I were allowed, I could tell you some stories about these two that would alarm them no end." She nodded toward the majors. "Several of them with well over ninety percent probability."

Henderson positively blanched, but Beale nodded. "That would not surprise me. Alice can be remarkably astute, Captain."

"So I see."

He stood and took his coffee cup over to the glass pot the waitress had left on a warmer plate when she'd taken breakfast order.

Daniel could see that his hands were not rock steady. Apparently the captain made the same observation of himself. He stopped pouring for a moment, took a deep breath, then finished the task with rock-steady hands. Captain Smith returned to the table and took his seat with a calm that almost belied the moment he'd needed to recover.

"And what remarkably astute observation has caused me to cross into U.S. territory for such an eclectic conference?"

Daniel had thought about sliding up to the subject carefully, to test the man out. But if Alice approved of Captain Smith, and he in turn was apparently coming 'round to appreciating Alice, perhaps he would forego that step.

"We need a meeting location."

The Captain did not state the obvious, that U.S. soil had thousands of locations just as obscure as the present one. He knew that he wouldn't have been contacted if that were the issue. He nodded for Daniel to continue.

"As I'm sure you just surmised, it cannot be on U.S. soil. Yet we want it to be very near. It must have immense security that can be implemented by a minimal force."

"As the White House Chief of Staff is seated across the table from me, I can assume some measure of the care required. Though your lack of Secret Service escort must be truly irritating someone back in Washington, D.C. Does that also speak to the scale of your ultimate operational requirements?" The Captain waited with that amazing stillness Daniel had witnessed in so many of the Special Forces best operators.

Highest security was required for this mission. And with each person they added, that needed secrecy became less reliable. Daniel nodded toward the flight crew presently in the room.

"This is it. Full team. Maximum protection. Maximum." He let the last word hang.

The Captain whistled quietly.

Achieving a truly high-level protection force with only four people was a contradiction of terms. A simple bodyguard detail even for Daniel would normally be two or three. The President's public visits, between advance site prep, security, press, and so on, often exceeded five hundred people not counting local law enforcement for crowd control. President Clinton had once planned to visit the African nation of Burkina Faso. They'd had to cancel when the advance team determined that there were insufficient hotel rooms in existence in the entire capital city of Ouagadougou to accommodate the President's full entourage.

"We're the site approval and inspection team. I doubt there will be many more for the meeting itself." Daniel tried not to think about that. "A day of site prep. Probably two nights and one day on site."

"Don't suppose you're going to tell me who will be visiting?"

Daniel glanced at Alice for a moment.

After a hesitation, she nodded her head.

Daniel could feel his shoulders ache as if he'd just done fifty reps with too much weight. Every single thing Alice had said so far had played out. From the arms smugglers in Pakistan, to Captain Nathaniel Smith, to the back check that North Korea actually would be sending someone.

Except for the absolute impossibility of the situation, he had no reason to doubt her next conclusion either. North Korea's Supreme Leader Kim Jong-Un was leaving the safety of his country to meet privately with the President of the United States.

Alice reaffirmed the nod more certainly. Brushing her hair aside to glare at him without even the partial screen of her bangs.

Daniel resisted the urge to sigh. This grew trickier by the minute.

"We're unsure," he had to decide how completely to trust the Captain. He hadn't even told Majors Beale and Henderson yet about Alice's conclusions. Need to know. Well, to keep the President safe, they now needed to know. All three of them. He took a deep breath and forged on, keeping his voice low.

"I wouldn't be shocked if we were hosting two heads of state."

That caused enough reaction at the table for the two crew chiefs seated at the far end of the room to spring to their feet and slip hands onto their sidearms.

Beale recovered first and waved for them to stand down.

Tim and Big John returned to their seats very slowly. But not until they performed a careful scan of the room, out the window to the sparsely used parking lot, and down the stairs to where the lone morning waitress was waiting for the breakfast order to be cooked. They finally settled back into their chairs.

Daniel turned back to face Captain Smith and the Majors. Daniel offered a slow nod as confirmation that he too believed the assessment.

The Captain didn't need to know which other country was involved. The fact that the U.S. President would likely be holding a secret meeting on Canadian soil with a tiny security detail was already too much information.

The Majors had obviously reached other conclusions based on their deeper knowledge of the situation. They looked even more sober than usual. They'd been ready to fly into North Korea. That hadn't fazed them for a moment. That they might well be transporting Kim Jong-un, the country's Supreme Leader, was a different matter entirely.

The chill remained only half a moment longer.

By the stairs, one of the crew chiefs scraped his chair back loudly sending a clear signal. The cheery waitress climbed the stairs wielding a large tray piled with dishes. The smells of a hot breakfast reminded Daniel that all he'd had in the last twenty-four hours was a quick sandwich at his desk and a finger-sized candy cane.

Everyone slipped into casual-mode so easily that Daniel had trouble crediting the room's tension from a moment before.

"Did you ever sail among the San Juan Islands, Alice?" Captain Smith asked it as if they had been discussing nothing but sailing for the last half hour.

Right in character, she shook her head, rested her elbow on the table, and propped her chin on her hand. So attentive she appeared to be flirting. Daniel was a little surprised at the hot trickle of jealousy up his spine despite his mind knowing the reaction to be ridiculous.

"I really prefer the Canadian Gulf Islands myself," Smith waved a negligent hand out the window and toward the northwest using the excuse to slouch a little closer to Alice. "Quiet up there. Fewer folk, on and off the water. There's this little bakery in Pender Harbor, fresh baked sourdough every morning. Whenever I sail in there, I buy a loaf and a stick of butter. That bread alone is as fine a meal as they set in any landside restaurant. No offense, ma'am," he nodded to the waitress.

"None taken. I've had that bread when we've gone up gunkholing on our little boat." She turned to Alice. "Fine eating if you get the chance, Miss."

"Gunkholing?"

"Definitely not from 'round about here. Gunkholing is, well, it's just puttering around for the hell of it. Pardon my language."

Daniel took a deep inhale and let it out slowly as he received his two eggs over easy on English muffins with hash browns and bacon.

When the waitress finally left, after regaling them the best way to cook fresh Dungeness crab on the boat barbeque, Smith returned them to the main topic.

"There is a little island that should interest you. A tad bit over eighty kilometers to the northwest. Privately-owned island. A single building. Non-resident owner. Only access is by air, unless you have the control code for the dock crane. That will better explain itself when viewed in person. High cliffs, large front lawn. Trees and, at this time of year, a truly deep sense of privacy. Not many fools sailing the channels in mid-December."

"How well known?" Major Beale asked.

"Not very," Smith dug a fork into his tall stack with bacon and sausage. "When the joker who built the crazy place was looking for an on-call helicopter service, he wanted the very best. Ended up calling a buddy of mine, retired SAS pilot who had moved from Glasgow to open a small Vancouver helicopter service. Flies for him, and still does the odd flight for me to keep his hand in."

He turned to the majors, "Either of you ever flown with James McKee?"

Emily Beale burst out laughing. "Tried to pick me up in the midst of a deep-ocean search and rescue operation back when I was a first lieutenant and he was a charming son-of-a-bitch freshly done with wife number four."

"Yes," Smith smiled. "That would be James. You're his type, doesn't surprise me."

"What?" Beale asked. "Female?"

Smith laughed. "Exactly. Also he's very partial to a woman who flies. Regrettably he's on vacation to see his second or maybe it's his third set of kids. They're in London."

"Do we need him?" Major Henderson's voice was little more than a growl. His protectiveness of his wife, even for events long before they met, made Daniel feel less bad about his own reaction of jealousy about Alice.

"Don't need him for a second," Smith offered. "All you need is the ten numbers of the security code, which I happen to know."

Chapter 24

They unpacked one of the Black Hawks from the C-17.

Alice watched from inside the cavernous cargo bay of the transport jet as the crew chiefs hauled one of the helicopters down the rear ramp and out into the chill rain. It required the better part of thirty minutes for Tim and John to unfold the rotor blades and prepare for flight. The Majors had spent about ten minutes circling the bird doing the external preflight checks before moving into the cockpit. Captain Smith had tagged along and now squatted just behind the pilots' seats, clearly talking shop.

They were all acting as if it were a normal day. Perhaps it was for them. Alice was ready to find the nearest walk-in freezer to warm up. It was merely freezing in Washington, D.C. The Pacific Northwest weather had supplied a slanting rain that was several degrees warmer and felt twice as cold. Even though she'd been sitting dry inside the belly of the C-17, she could feel the cold wind as it tested and probed the entire length of the cargo bay through the open rear ramp.

Daniel stood outside too, the hood of his parka up. Not quite in the way, but not out of it either. Clearly enjoying being a guy around other guys doing guy things. He'd watched as they pinned the rotor blades in place. Once they showed him how, he'd tossed a line over the ends of the long rotor blades that had been tucked over the tail. He towed each one so that Tim and John who were perched atop the Black Hawk could pin them into place. Then as the crew chiefs worked their way around the bird undoing covers, checking door latches, and a hundred other little details, Daniel asked questions.

Alice would bet that he didn't forget a single detail either. Every item finding its cubbyhole in his neatly ordered mind. Her own mind felt more like a filing system crossed with a smallish hurricane. Her ability to retrieve and relate facts remained a constant mystery whenever she tried to explore her own process. Daniel didn't appear to go there. His mind, while at least as exceptional as his body, appeared to be something he simply used. Didn't analyze. Didn't deconstruct. He just used it.

Sounded like a nice, gentle place to be. She wished she could try it someday.

They finally waved her over and she scampered through the rain. Only Daniel's quick hand atop her head spared her cracking it on the cargo bay doorframe. The Black Hawk's deck was a high step up, but the bay itself measured barely over four feet from deck to roof of the cabin. A couple of small seats had been attached there, three across the back facing forward and two at the front facing backward.

She and Daniel took two of the seats in the back. He patted the middle seat and she slid in gratefully, as far as possible from the freezing outside world and able to rub shoulders with Daniel.

Captain Smith sat across from them.

The two crew chiefs went forward and took their own positions after sliding the cargo bay door shut. They rode sideways, each facing out a small window. The windows actually only appeared small. Each was mostly filled with a steerable minigun capable of firing six thousand rounds a minute, a buzz saw of death.

A shiver having nothing to do with the temperature shook Alice so hard it almost hurt. Never had it been so personal, seeing the danger she was placing people in. She rarely left her cubicle at CIA headquarters. She'd make an analysis, and people would act on it. These people, ones she now knew, would fly into harm's way because of what she'd learned. They were sitting in a craft of war. And this time her analysis would be sending them into North Korea.

The majors closed their own doors and within moments the twin turbines had spun up until they were a high background whine, a sound she knew would be in her sleep for days to come. The heavy thud of the rotors began to beat the air hard enough that it felt like a body blow.

With a deepening of the rotor's roar and a slight forward tip, they were airborne. Within moments they were over water, barely, but above it. She knew that Puget Sound was close to the south end of the runway, but she knew they were supposed to heading northwest. Maybe they were circling around to make sure no one had their trail. At twenty-feet above the curling winter whitecaps of Bellingham Bay, no radar would be following them.

Daniel slid an arm over her shoulder, but there was no way to talk. She leaned in for the warmth and comfort, and watched the world flash by out the large windows in the closed cargo doors. Steep islands appeared abruptly, stabbing their conifer-covered heads briefly toward the sky before sweeping back toward the roiled ocean waters. They slalomed between the islands as smoothly as any ice skater, at least one dumb enough to be gliding a half second above instant death. If they caught a wave at this speed they'd be dead before even the best pilots could react.

Somehow the impossibility of the situation didn't worry her. Whatever the fates had in store, they were in control at the moment. Not Alice Thompson. Not even a little.

With Daniel's arm warm about her, she felt safe. She felt for the first time as if she belonged.

The brilliant outsider, the analyst that no one could feel comfortable around, faded away. The one that everyone assumed could see right through them. But she couldn't. She didn't understand individuals, herself least of all. Politics, sure. Socio-economic dynamics of battle, no problem. What the guy next to her was thinking, never. At least not until Daniel.

She lay her head against his shoulder and soon fell asleep in the safest place she'd ever known.

Chapter 25

Daniel didn't hear any change to the helicopter's rotors, but Captain Smith signaled they were nearing their destination.

He wanted to tell Beale and Henderson to just keep flying. To never stop. Alice asleep inside the curl of his arm, her hair soft, brushing his cheek.

The Canadian Gulf Islands out the window looked wilder than the American San Juans. The forests had fewer breaks for houses. Roads were narrow lanes rather than stretches of well-paved-and-striped two-ways. Fifty miles northwest of the airport and they'd also illegally crossed an international border.

He shook Alice gently awake. There was no way over the rotor noise, but he'd swear he could hear a hum of contentment from Alice as she turned her face into his shoulder.

Daniel hesitated because Captain Smith sat there facing them from two feet away.

Screw it.

He brushed Alice's chin upward with a soft caress and then kissed her awake.

Half awake, she leaned in; soft, warm, slow, luscious.

Daniel's seatbelt was abruptly too tight across his lap in exactly the wrong place.

When fully awake, there was no sudden hesitancy. As if she knew even in her sleep exactly who she was kissing. Sitting here, in a roaring helicopter, might well be the sexiest moment of his life. Not for any of his body's happy imaginings about sex, but for the familiar sensuality in Alice Thompson's kiss.

The helicopter banked and Daniel glanced up to see a daunting cliff wall very close outside the window.

"Holy wow!" Alice's observation was just audible.

Thirty or forty feet high, the cliffs soared straight out of the pounding waves. The water must be deep because no pile of boulders huddled around the base. Anything that broke free here was headed for deep water. A steady turn lasted them through a full 360-degree circuit around the island. All cliff.

Then the majors flew the chopper upward on a second circuit around the perimeter. Tall stands of dark, dark evergreen trees capped the rugged island that couldn't be much over a quarter-mile across. As they returned to the south side, an opening appeared in the forest.

A green lawn notched back into the trees. Near the cliff edge perched a massive metal-lattice crane. At the end of the crane dangled a floating dock, presently placed on the high meadow. Clearly, you could show up in your boat, engage the remote control, and swing the dock down to the water forty feet below for moorage. A long walkway dangled from the lower side of the crane boom, creating a bridge from ship to shore when it was in position.

Of course, right now, you'd have to be suicidal to brave the roiled winter waters.

Upslope, beyond the crane, a helipad had been leveled out in the middle of the yard. Even a bright orange windsock, which stood pointing like an angry finger to the north indicating a strong southerly wind despite the shielding trees.

At the head of the slope stood a very traditional stone house. The kind of house that would stand out even in an affluent neighborhood. Not for its size, though it wasn't small, but rather for an English elegance. Ivy had climbed up the lower third of the front, creating a sunshield over a deep porch facing the view.

Daniel lost the view as the chopper spun to face the wind and the wheels touched down on the helipad.

With the rotors still cranking, the crew chiefs piled out and tied the chopper down to the large iron rings sunk into the helipad's surface.

As the rotors finally wound down, and Daniel's ears popped in relief, they all piled out into the roaring wind beneath a sky of crystalline, winter-blue and just stood there staring at the house. It was impossible, unlikely, and absolutely perfect.

The house looked pleasant, stood on neutral soil, and could be secured by a minimal team.

"Damn! That's sweet." Alice's comment, barely louder than the wind, set them in motion across the lawn toward the house.

Chapter 26

One of the things Daniel had learned during his year as the White House Chief-of-Staff was that any concept of what he'd thought it meant to be busy was impossibly naïve. And in the week following the visit to the island house, it only got crazier. Seven days since his one-day trip across the country and back. He must have slept and eaten at some point, but right now he was far too tired to recall.

He slumped in his office chair.

Janet had somehow made room for a tiny Christmas tree, more of a Christmas bush, at the corner of this desk. A pine bough trim had been woven around the edges of the "Death Board;" a white board covered with the strategy to defeat a couple of exceptionally short-sighted bills put forth by the opposition party. A small tintype print of a dollhouse that he'd grown rather fond of had been replaced by a triptych of original Currier and Ives lithographs on loan from the Smithsonian.

Daniel closed his eyes and tried to catch up with the last week's events.

The island house had been toured, reviewed, and approved in under ten minutes. They'd ducked back across the border, thanked Captain Smith, and parted ways.

The Black Hawk crew departed to place their equipment and practice for the upcoming assignment. Daniel and Alice had found a small charter to take them to SeaTac airport. At D.C. they'd gone their separate ways and found even less time to be together over this week than the prior one, if that was even possible.

The inner circle on this operation was impossibly small which meant that practically everything had to be done by Daniel himself. That was above and beyond all of the work that came from the tail end of the pre-Holiday session in Congress.

In the last forty-eight hours he'd brokered peace and an acceptable approval margin on bills in education and farming. He'd failed on border and immigration controls, but the President had wrangled that one to the ground by a three-vote squeak in the House and two in the Senate. A win was a win, no matter how close, but it had left both of them strung out and exhausted.

Meanwhile, preparation for the upcoming North Korean operation continued. Beale and Henderson had moved their two Black Hawks into position.

Alice managed to push a message back up the chain to let their mystery guest know the plan once the Majors had finished formulating and rehearsing it.

The head of the PPD, the Secret Service's Presidential Protection Detail, Agent Frank Adams, had been brought into the inner circle.

Frank had headed the detail since the President had first polled in the double digits, long before he was nominated. Frank had ridden herd on three Presidents and dozens of VIPs in his twenty-plus years in the service.

He had protested vehemently when not allowed to add another agent, or preferably an entire division. And when the head of the PPD protested, in that gravelly deep voice of his, and all six-two of him looming over Daniel, instant death in an immaculate black business suit, he paid attention.

Daniel had thought Adams would lock the President in the Oval Office. And maybe just shoot Daniel for good measure. Then the President had mentioned that Major Emily Beale was involved. In that instant the tone of the meeting changed entirely and Frank Adams was on board.

Daniel was left to puzzle over that abrupt change. As far as he knew the only time they'd met was when the First Lady had been killed and the animosity between them at the time had been unmistakable. Daniel tried to get Frank aside on the subject, but he was as mute as the Secret Service always was about security matters.

The one person Daniel never saw outside of strategy meetings was Dr. Alice Thompson. And that was killing him. She'd taken to texting him after the third time he'd fallen asleep with the phone to his ear, while they were talking.

"What's in the calendar tonight?" she asked one night.

"Cinnamon Bears. Spicy!"

"Drink milk."

And milk had worked to soothe the burning heat that had been boring a hole through his tongue.

"Spice drops tonight."

"Christmas wish," she'd texted whatever that night was. "I want to be there to kiss you."

"Sour ones."

"I take back my Christmas wish. Well, not really."

Back and forth by phone and text as the entire middle page of the Advent calendar was emptied door by tiny door.

December 17th. Daniel slumped in his chair, ragged with exhaustion. It took concerted effort to reach out his arm and pull the Advent Calendar off the top of a mountain of vetting folders for a new Supreme Court justice. Arnold Johnson had let them know he'd be announcing his retirement on the first of the year and the scramble was on to choose President Matthews' first replacement on the high court.

Daniel's phone buzzed as he pulled the calendar into his lap. He dragged it out and had to blink several times before his eyes would focus on the message.

"What's the third picture?"

Of course Alice would notice and keep track. Three page spreads, twenty-four days, hence eight days per page. December 17th, the start of page three of the Advent calendar.

He untied the red ribbon and carefully unfolded the book to inspect the interior.

Page one, loading the sleigh.

Page two, the Christmas Hamster leaving the gifts under the tree in such bounty they spilled across the floor.

Page three. He had to stop a moment and catch his breath. It was simply that beautiful.

"What is it?" Alice's text buzzed his phone again.

"It's us." Daniel hit send before he quite realized what he'd done. He looked desperately for an "untext" option, but there wasn't one. Besides, it was true. It was an image that had been forming slowly in his head. Building in quiet layers without his noticing until he saw the image of it spread before him. An image of his life as he couldn't quite see it yet. Or rather hadn't until he opened the page. It was how "home" was meant to be.

"Show me."

"Wish I could," he sent back. But he had hours of work before he'd have a chance of going to bed, never mind time to see Alice.

"Show me."

Daniel hit reply on the phone, but something didn't look right. That's when it registered that he'd heard the last comment, not read it.

He looked up and there she sat across from him, slouched in his chair, red-and-green checked sneakers propped on the edge of his desk. A bountifully soft-looking sweater in palest gold wrapped her like a warm embrace.

When he looked into her eyes, her soft, hazeled, smiling eyes, his phone buzzed sharply.

Habit, he couldn't help himself, he glanced down.

"Show me."

When he looked back up, she raised her hand from below his line of sight and revealed her phone.

He handed across the calendar.

She took it and set it across her lap without sitting up.

Daniel slumped back in his chair and watched Alice as she viewed the final picture on the calendar.

Her bangs had slid down over her eyes but he could see the softness enter her body in the rounding of the shoulders, the cool hand placed against a cheek perhaps suddenly too warm, and finally the palm of her hand rested over her heart.

She looked at it for a long, long time. Then she closed it slowly, as if it were delicate and precious and held it to her chest wrapped in both arms for a moment. She stood and placed it on top of the most stable stack on his desk and circled around to him.

Alice didn't speak. She didn't kiss him. She simply held out a hand. When he took it, she pulled him inexorably to his feet.

In silence, she led him through the twisting passages of the West Wing and the White House. Only when they arrived in his bedroom on the third floor of the Residence, did she speak.

"Show me."

Chapter 27

Alice woke alone. Knew she was alone in Daniel's four-poster bed without even opening her eyes.

She knew she shouldn't be surprised, but it hurt anyway.

Toughen up, Thompson. You're used to this.

She was. Most men she'd ever dated left before daybreak. Left her alone in her bed or even stranger, alone in theirs. Over time she'd gone out on fewer and fewer dates. And become more and more selective on who passed through the first date successfully, never mind through her door.

Somehow Daniel strode through her barricades from the moment she saw him in that three-piece suit befuddled by an Advent calendar.

Last night had been another voyage into amazing, mind-bending sex. Yet now she woke alone.

She opened one eye to inspect the dent in the navy blue flannel-covered pillow beside her.

No note.

No flower.

Nothing.

She rubbed at her eyes with the heels of her hands and let out a frustrated growl. When the hell was she going to learn?

Time to get moving.

She sat up, the sheets sliding into her lap and one bare leg stretched out to snag her underwear from the floor, when she heard the door open.

"Holy shit!" Daniel's voice was low and hoarse.

He stood barefoot, his shirt partially buttoned, wrong by two button-holes, and a pair of pants with the belt undone and riding low on those delicious hips. He held a large tray that he was dangerously close to bobbling onto the hardwood floor.

It had a single flower in a slender-necked crystal vase. A red rose. And a breakfast spread that could kill her. The man had cooked for her. It smelled glorious.

"Hold it." Alice thought back through their various conversations. "You never swear."

"I also don't often see the Goddess Venus rising naked from my bed. And I do, too, swear."

"Never heard it." Alice pulled the sheet back up to her neck, and slid her leg back under the covers fighting a blush as hard as she could. At least Daniel had regained control of the tray.

"I don't swear around you."

"Why?"

"You're a lady."

Alice laughed. "No, I'm not!"

Daniel straightened in ire, clearly ready to leap to her defense. His control-of-tray skills once again drifted dangerously toward loss. Not with her flower on it. She scooted forward, trying to trap the sheet across her body with her chin as she rescued the tray. It sort of worked, only one breast was exposed by the time she'd maneuvered the tray to the bed and had the vase safely cradled in her hands.

"Who says you aren't a lady?" He was truly indignant on her behalf.

She let the sheet drop and held her arms out to the sides, careful to keep the rose upright. "Hello, naked in your bed. For the second time. We met less than two weeks ago."

"More than. Sixteen days, five hours, and thirty-eight minutes." He barely hesitated to check the bedside clock.

Alice reached for the sheet again. "What am I going to do with you?" She also knew it to the minute, but that was simply how her mind worked. She certainly hadn't expected him to as well. He kept charming her, even when she didn't want to be.

"Well, I could make a few suggestions, but your breakfast would be cold."

It was long gone cold when they finally got around to eating it.

Chapter 28

Alice was tying his tie as he buttoned her blouse. Such a damn gentleman he didn't even feel up the woman he'd just spent most of the night ravaging, and not so many minutes ago slathering with a soapy washcloth in the shower.

"There actually was a reason I came by last night."

He leaned in and kissed her so slowly and gently, as if he had all day rather than a mere six minutes to get to his first meeting of the day.

"Nice, Dr. Darlington. Really, really nice." Alice tried not to sigh like a schoolgirl. "But that wasn't it."

"Oh, well, worth a try."

"Try again…"

He leaned back in eager as a teenager.

"Later." She managed to complete her sentence and place a hand on his chest in time to stop his forward motion. If he kissed her like that again she'd be dragging him back to bed whether or not the Minority Whip was waiting for him.

"They've decided to take the Black Hawks?"

Daniel was sharp enough that he didn't even blink at the topic change. "Yes. The Majors believe they can fly a lower profile with the Hawks than in the Hound. And the Mil Hound simply didn't have the necessary reactive ability if the situation became sticky."

"Picture it. The new leader of North Korea, a clandestine meeting, and a military helicopter."

"It's probably expected."

"Filled with military personnel..." Alice let her words drag out.

Daniel only hesitated a moment longer before offering a low whistle.

"I didn't see that." He straightened her sweater and her blouse, fussing with the collar, but clearly his mind was somewhere else.

"A civilian needs to be there for the ride." Alice did her best to make it a perfectly neutral statement.

"And that someone is?"

Alice didn't like her answer. Didn't like the image of that helicopter risking its way into North Korea, opening a door into unknown danger, and the man stepping out was...

"Me." Daniel's face went white as he answered his own question. "Oh man. Now I really wish I did swear."

Chapter 29

"You promise you aren't going to kill me?" Daniel had to shout to be heard over the noise on the deck of the aircraft carrier.

"Nuh-uh! No such promises." Major Beale was practically laughing at him and Daniel had no recourse.

He was only so much baggage. Had been for the last twenty hours.

Civilian transport had moved him from Dulles to Tokyo over the pole. Then a quick transport had shuffled him down to Kadena Air Base on Okinawa. Thirty minutes later, a Marine Corps V-22 Osprey, only recently authorized to operate over Japanese soil, lifted him into international waters and dropped him on the deck of the aircraft carrier U.S.S. Harry S. Truman at close to midnight.

Beale and Henderson had awaited him there. The Sea of Japan was in a very bad mood tonight. Waves strong enough to roll the carrier's deck by several feet rushed by unseen in the darkness below. The wind cast nasty ice particles at his face; cast the same way a machine gun cast bullets, continuous and painful.

The group of them as much blew into as climbed aboard the waiting Black Hawk.

"Is this safe flying weather?" he listened to the rattle of the ice against the cargo bay door windows once they were closed and he could hear himself think.

Big John, one of the crew chiefs, flashed a grin at him from where he somehow had mashed into the tiny seat set up for the crew chiefs.

"When the post office gives it up as a bad job, we do their deliveries."
Great.

Tim handed him a helmet and suggested he buckle in as the turbine engines began whining to life. Outside he could see the organized scurry of the deck crew preparing to receive an incoming jet and launch their helicopter. All their vests color-coded by their tasks. The deck was not awash in a blaze of light as he'd expected. For night operations, they didn't want to blind the pilots, so lights were low and carefully positioned.

Inside the chopper there was actually very little to see. Daniel sat in one of the three seats across the back of the cabin. Cabin, a glorious word for a space four feet high and perhaps eight-by-eight feet inside. He tried to imagine it crammed with a dozen troops and all their gear and couldn't imagine it. Of course, the major's helicopter was an attack version, so carrying crew would be less of a priority.

At the very front of the cabin the two crew chiefs sat back-to-back. Immediately in front of them were closed windows. Daniel knew they could swing those windows aside in moments and grasp the controls of the mini-guns rigged there. For now, they were just passive travelers, any information they might need projected on the inside of their visors.

Daniel's visor was clear. A "dummies helmet" he'd been informed. They didn't want to be revealing any more than they had to for their North Korean guest. Henderson figured it would be more politic if Daniel wore the same thing they had. Clear plastic, audio hookup only. And an emergency locator beacon if they had to ditch in the ocean.

What in the world had he gotten himself into?

Straight ahead, between the two armor-wrapped seats, Daniel could see only the dimmest of console lights. They were rigged to be used with the pilots' night-vision goggles; no extra light. There was little variation inside the cabin whether Daniel opened or closed his eyes.

The rotor blades were at full speed now, pounding the night air with the ferocity of a rabid dog.

Daniel contemplated his chances for survival. Storms, aircraft carriers, helicopters at night, North Korea. And he knew that if he lived there were things he'd have to do. One especially. He sent a quick message from his cell phone to set them in motion.

He managed to hit "send" as they jolted rather than lifted into the night sky. Once they crossed over the edge of the carrier's windswept deck, the chopper plunged abruptly down toward the black of the deep ocean.

Daniel's yelp was going to be the last sound of his life before the waves swallowed him. He wished he'd told Alice. He wasn't sure what, he just wished he had.

He should have sent the text to her instead.

Too late!

With a twist and jerk that elicited another cry he couldn't quite contain, the helicopter's nose tipped forward and they raced ahead.

Daniel leaned over to glance backward out the side window. The aircraft carrier rapidly disappearing astern. Before it wholly disappeared from view, he was able to guess that they were skimming ten or twenty feet above the waves.

"Damn. It. Emily!" It took him two gasping breathes and a dozen racing beats of his heart to get out the three words.

"Sorry, Daniel." Her voice didn't sound in the least contrite. "We didn't want any radar image to show a flight departing westbound. Rather than circling around, we decided to lose ourselves in the clutter cast up by waves and spray."

"You're making me feel so much better."

Daniel decided his best bet was to ignore her. And her husband. He could feel Mark's grin even though he faced forward in the left-hand pilot's seat.

"Left seat? I thought pilot flew right seat on military helicopters." Mark was the senior commanding officer.

"Yep!" Mark replied in a terrible Texas drawl. "My little lady likes to drive and who am I to complain?"

Future note for self, Daniel thought, *this helmet mikes picked up even an idle whisper.* Henderson had to be one brave man to call Major Emily Beale, "my little lady." Daniel would bet that even her father didn't take such risks. He knew the President, her closest childhood friend, certainly didn't take such liberties.

"Okay, now it gets interesting. Entering Russian airspace."

"Russian?" Daniel tried looking out the window, but only darkness met his gaze. Away from the carrier, the only light glimmered from the dim console instruments. Unseen waves below, solid overcast above, nasty storm in between. All pitch black.

Henderson continued his commentary as his wife flew the helicopter. "Even in bad weather, North Korea watches their waters pretty closely. There's a risk crossing over a land border, but perhaps less of a risk."

"How much longer is the flight because of the detour?"

"Just a few minutes. Thirty minutes each way total if all goes well."

Daniel wished he'd started a timer on his watch, though it was buried under parka and heavy gloves that barely cut the December cold.

The carrier had been steaming south through the Sea of Japan. That would also draw most of the region's attention with it. It wasn't often that a full carrier group cruised this particular stretch of the world's oceans.

"Feet dry," Beale announced.

At least they were over land now and clear of any rogue wave that might be reaching out to grab them.

Then the chopper banked hard left, jerked up and dropped back down. Daniel floated for a moment in the chair's safety harness, then slapped back down into his seat.

"Sometimes it gets a little rough," Big John observed in a laconic voice suitable for a summer picnic, "but this storm's mostly out to sea, so it should be a quiet flight."

The helicopter threw him sideways against his harness as it tipped right then left.

"Just got to watch out for trees and things."

"Cows," was Emily Beale's sole offering to the conversation.

Daniel thought about the implications and then just closed his eyes against the darkness.

They were flying so low that she had to maneuver to avoid the cows.

Chapter 30

The chopper pulled sharply nose up and Daniel felt that forward motion had ceased.

At some point in the flight, he had dropped into a meditative fog, letting the chopper simply fling his body back-and-forth as it deemed fit. He'd stopped thinking of the long flight since D.C., of the travesty he'd be faced with for having been several days away from his desk. He didn't even think of Alice much. Not as some separate thought. She simply nestled there in the corner of his mind. Giving him a reason to come out of this alive.

It took him a moment to tune into the report that Major Henderson was giving.

"Small building, perhaps five or six rooms. Two outbuildings. Only one vehicle. Coordinates and conditions match. Drone shows no other heat signatures within three miles, though it is not a good night for observing."

Drone. A remote-controlled drone must be patrolling the area, forty pounds of plane flitting through the overhead clouds taking quick peeks below with its infrared camera.

Daniel managed to pull off his gloves and slide up his sleeve enough to see his watch. They were ten seconds from the time that Beale had insisted they'd be arriving. How she nailed ten seconds after a half hour flight across unknown terrain was a good trick indeed.

"Rolling in slow," Emily announced.

The crew chiefs opened their side windows and leaned out. Neither actively grasping the handles of the mounted guns, but he could see them poised to do so.

Daniel unclipped his belt and moved forward between the crew chiefs until he crouched between the pilot's seats. Through the front windshield, he could see very little. A small house, a porch light.

The porch door opened and Emily brought the helicopter to a halt once again, now hovering barely a hundred feet from the building.

One figure stood on the stoop and scanned the night. Clearly hearing the Black Hawk, but having trouble seeing it, a blacked-out bird on a foul night.

A second figure joined the first, a machine gun held across his chest, pointed toward the sky. The second figure took only a moment to pinpoint them in the dark and swing his rifle to bear on their position.

That the second man held a small rifle and Daniel sat behind a bullet-proof windshield in one of the toughest weaponized vehicles ever sent to war, did little to calm his nerves.

"I thought you said just one." Beale's question was clearly meant for him.

Daniel considered Alice's final conclusion during the briefing she'd given him in the back of the car as he'd been driven to the airport.

"If the first man is who we think it is, the guy with the gun is probably his version of Frank Adams."

"You better be right about this." Beale began easing the helicopter forward. "Be real quiet about it boys, but be ready for steel."

Daniel wanted to protest. He knew what that meant. They were in a DAP Hawk, a Direct Action Penetrator Black Hawk, the nastiest weapons platform ever launched into the night sky. The DAP's motto was "We Deal in Steel." A call for "Steel" meant the unleashing of a nearly unimaginable amount of firepower.

But it wasn't his flight. He was only there for the meet-and-greet moment, not for the danger of fifty million dollars worth of highly classified weapon invading the planet's single most paranoid nation.

Beale eased forward until the rotor was mere feet from the eaves of the house and settled to the manicured lawn. Daniel could feel that she was barely letting the wheels touch, still technically flying and ready to maneuver at a moment's notice.

She left the choppers nose pointed directly at the two men on the porch. All weapons to bear.

"You're on, Ace." Henderson leaned into the space between the pilots' seats and nodded his helmet in Daniel's direction.

Right. He moved toward the cargo bay door being opened by one of the crew chiefs, Tim Maloney. Tim snapped a line to the large ring on the front of the vest they'd made Daniel put on.

"In case we have to bug out quickly. Wouldn't want to be leaving you behind."

Daniel stepped down onto the hard-frozen ground and tried not to picture himself dangling beneath a speeding helicopter, then accidentally being smashed into the side of a stray cow.

He stopped at half the distance to the two men, at the limit of his tether, doing his best to ignore the rotors spinning just three feet over his head. They'd told him not to raise his hand above his head if he chose to wave.

He and the two men held the tableau for the better part of thirty seconds. Daniel seriously considered giving the bug-out signal that they'd taught him.

Then the man without the machine gun came forward. He was silhouetted by the porch light behind him. Not until he stopped just a pace away was Daniel able to see his face.

Alice had been absolutely right.

Daniel reached out his right hand to greet North Korea's Supreme Leader, the Supreme Commander of her Army's and the First Secretary of the Communist Party, Kim Jong-Un.

Chapter 31

The guard had come up close behind the leader.

Kim spoke in rapid Korean. His bodyguard translated, "With who do we meet? You do not look military." By the way he eyed the helicopter, Daniel decided it was a good thing he had come along. In the dim glow of the porch light, with her rotors spinning just an arm's reach overhead, the Black Hawk looked lethal and ready to pounce at the slightest provocation; a mad dog barely chained.

"Daniel Drake Darlington, White House Chief of Staff. At your service."

Another back and forth.

It might have been his imagination, but both men appeared to relax even before the translation began. How good was the leader's English? His file said educated in Switzerland. That meant German and probably French.

"And with who do we meet? And where?"

Daniel wanted to glance back at the helicopter for support, but he knew they were the ones waiting for him.

"I come bearing an invitation from President of the United States Peter Matthews to meet with him on a quiet and secure island in British Columbia, Canada. Other than myself and the four aboard the helicopter behind me, there will only be two others. Only two other people on the planet know about this." Captain Smith was one. And the Vice President had been briefed in the event of foul play.

After waiting for the translation, the two men looked at each other. Daniel could feel his heart beat once, twice, three times. Then, with no signal that Daniel could discern, the one with the machine gun returned to the house, turned off the porch light plunging them into near-total darkness, and closed the door. When he returned, they indicated that Daniel should lead the way.

In sixty seconds the three of them were helmeted and strapped in side-by-side. In ten seconds more they were airborne. The flight then proceeded in perfect silence, not even any comments about the cow and tree dodging.

Not until twelve minutes away from the house.

Chapter 32

"We have a fast-sweep radar ahead." Henderson's comment was calm, uninflected.

"That's a problem. They weren't there when we were inbound." Beale had jerked them to a standstill.

Without asking, the crew chiefs had shoved open their access doors and had their hands on their miniguns.

"Did they hear us on our inbound leg?"

"We entered five clicks to the west. Unless they've lit up the whole border."

Daniel and the two Koreans leaned over to look out the cabin windows. Some vague glimmer of light revealed that they were hovering only a few feet above an open meadow. Trees ahead and to the side were visible as dark blotches in front of the stars.

"We have to climb to get out of here. Twenty-five feet at least. That will put us right in their eyes. All we're hearing now is the spillover and reflections. They won't have any signal on us yet."

The Koreans conversed briefly over the intercom and the guard spoke for the first time since boarding.

"Tests. Last five minutes, no more minutes. We conserve power, no continuous radar." He tried to speak proudly.

But Daniel could hear the bluff, read between the lines. Either they were unsophisticated enough to think that leaving them off most of the time meant they weren't known and mapped; unlikely. Or, more likely, they didn't have sufficient fuel to justify constant operation of the power draining equipment. North Korea had many problems, food and fuel shortages nearing the top of those lists.

Daniel started the lapse timer on his watch.

They knew Pyongyang was surrounded by more anti-aircraft guns than all other cities in the world combined. Over six hundred known sites surrounded the city. Hence their remote country meeting at one of Kim Jong-un's vacation retreats.

But the border was also guarded.

If the radar sweep spotted their helicopter, they might still get out, but they'd never manage to get the Supreme Leader back in with the whole country on alert for an invasion.

The guard started to speak and Daniel could see him waved to silence. He tried again, but finally relented at the sharpness of his leader's gesture.

So, they sat and waited.

Daniel stared at his watch through three minutes. Then four. Then five. He closed his eyes and did his best to not count in his head. To not think about the sheer mass of weaponry planted about them. North Korea's weaponry was old, but current estimates stated that they were so heavily armed they could throw over sixty-thousand tons of highly explosive shells into the air in the first minute.

"It has been seven minutes," Beale stated.

Daniel could feel the sweat soaking this palms, his forehead, his thoughts—murky, confused. His breath was short. Ragged.

"There we go." Henderson sounded cheerful enough that Daniel's thoughts of imminent death eased slightly.

"Sky reads clear. We'll give them another minute."

Daniel spent the very long sixty seconds blessing the people who had trained this flight crew and designed the equipment the used to keep him alive.

Chapter 33

Twenty-five minutes after they set off again, the Black Hawk again flew over the water. By forty minutes they sighted the aircraft carrier.

That's when Daniel told Henderson to send the prearranged signal. The signal that would confirm the previously arranged tour of airbases by the President. The Commander-in-Chief had hastily arranged to offer a personal delivery of pre-Christmas wishes to many of America's fliers.

A tour that conveniently started with Joint Base Lewis-McChord in Tacoma Washington. There, he could land to meet with the Air Force at McChord very publicly, and then quietly cross over to Fort Lewis on the other side of the street; the home of the 4th and 5th battalions of the SOAR 160th, the U.S. Army's Special Operations Aviation Regiment.

When they swooped up from the wave tops to land on the carrier's flight deck with the softest kiss despite the heavy winds the two Koreans came to life.

Daniel couldn't help but enjoy the excitement with which the leader of a country so heavily invested in military strength plastered himself to the rain-streaked window to watch a jet catapult into the night sky. The fighter jet shot aloft with a roar that shook the helicopter. Kim Jong-un's bodyguard was no less interested, for the first time forgetting his absolute vigilance to protect his Supreme Leader.

Even as they watched it disappear into the low cloud cover off to the left, a large battleship-gray jet came from the right, slammed into the deck, and trapped on one of the wires. Its wingspan dwarfed the fighter that had just launched upward, but it lacked the lethal look. It was long, sleek, and had curled tips on the ends of the wings. A Gulfstream passenger jet. Right on schedule.

It was the only idea they had come up with to mobilize their group. The U.S. didn't have any supersonic passenger jets. And with Kim Jong-un's insistence on not setting foot in most countries within a couple thousand mile radius, it had been the only solution to move them all together.

They had discussed putting each individual of the party into the backseat of a Hornet FA-18 two-seat supersonic trainer, but decided against it at the last minute. It would mean increasing the circle of people who knew about the operation and who was aboard. Not the Air Boss, nor the carrier's commander knew who was crossing their deck. They didn't know where the helicopter had gone, it had been flying even below the sophisticated systems of the carrier once it was more than a few miles out.

As soon as the passenger jet came to rest, she was swarmed by a crew. Tail hook restowed, the plane was dragged immediately to the catapult position. After their helicopter was tied down, no one had approached them. No one opened the Black Hawk's door.

Suddenly the carrier's deck was conspicuously clear.

"That's our cue." Henderson climbed down and slid open the cargo bay door. He offered the two Koreans rain slicks with large, overhanging hoods that hid their faces. It only took moments to escort their guests from the helicopter to the steps on the Gulfstream jet.

A fresh flight crew would already be in place in the cockpit with specific instructions not to enter the main cabin short of an emergency. They even had the door itself closed off while boarding so they couldn't see who entered.

The crew chiefs, Tim and John, settled in the forward crew cabin right behind the entry door as if seeking privacy from the rear cabin, but actually guarding against any curiosity by the flight crew.

As Daniel followed the group last up the fold-down steps, a gust of freezing rain found its way down his neck.

Beale hit the door-close switch and Daniel walked through the short crew cabin and entered the main area. There were two groups of four arm chairs set in facing pairs on either side of a central aisle. Half had their backs to him, half facing him. At the far end a couch ran alongside one wall of the cabin facing across the plane to a fair-sized television. The entire cabin was dressed with white leather chairs and wall coverings. The trim and carpeting were charcoal gray.

Daniel scanned the cabin quickly. Per instructions, there was no sign of Christmas. In 2011, North Korea had threatened to shell a hundred-foot tall steel Christmas tree that shown over the border from South Korea. The President and Daniel had both recalled the escalating tension and decided to avoid it as much as possible. The aircraft carrier, involved in night operations, had no visible Christmas lights anyway.

Henderson was directing the Supreme Leader and his guard to take seats facing forward for the take-off. Right. Catapult-assisted takeoff. Sit on the couch and you'd end up spilled off the end and into the rear galley and probably right on into the small lavatory.

Beale and Henderson sat down in a forward pair of facing seats, leaving Daniel the last forward-facing armchair for the takeoff. He dropped into it with deep appreciation, closing his eyes in relief as he settled into the soft leather. He'd been traveling for almost twenty hours so far, and there was eight more to go to get back to Canada.

And the adrenal crash from hovering for nine long minutes in the midst of anti-aircraft radar systems had taken what little reserves he'd had.

Had he really served a purpose? He'd have to assume that the Supreme Leader of North Korea would not be seated right behind him at the moment if he hadn't gone. So, it had been a good decision, even if he was too tired to appreciate it.

The twin jets of the Gulfstream wound to life with a pleasantly muffled, high whine of a well-insulated passenger jet, rather than the mind-numbing roar of most military aircraft.

The engine's whine built and the pilot warned them to buckle up. Daniel groped around, clipped himself in and sank further into the seat. Exhaustion rolled over him like a wave.

He had done well. He'd survived a flight with Emily Beale, perhaps too busy worrying to actually be concerned with whatever near death experiences she'd been handing out in flight. Against all odds, they'd pulled off an impossible assignment, or at least the first half. Alice's guiding hand of knowledge and risk assessment had been flawless from the moment she'd walked into Daniel's office just three weeks before.

Three weeks. How did a world get so turned over in three weeks?

His world had become divided: before and after Advent calendar. Before and after meeting Alice. He'd thought the big change was his journey to Washington D.C. three years ago. Starting as champion of the Slow Food movement and the farming community of Tennessee. Becoming assistant to the First Lady and ultimately the White House Chief of Staff. How could any change in his life have surpassed that crazy set of circumstances? He'd thought that anything past serving President Matthews was bound to be a letdown.

The engine's roar increased until finally it was a palpable pressure in the cabin.

He'd been wrong though, the before and after moment that mattered was December first and a tiny door bearing the golden number "1" in finest filigree. That and a russet-haired beauty who'd turned his life upside down.

Someone patted him on the knee and he heard a soft, "Good job!" over the peaking roar of the engines.

The pilot warned over the intercom, "Launch in three."

Not takeoff. Launch.

He opened his eyes and there, like a miracle, sat Alice.

He opened his mouth to exclaim his shock just as the catapult fired ramming him hard back into the seat and driving out what little air had survived in his lungs.

Chapter 34

"I thought I might be useful." Alice had pulled off the conveniently padded strap that had slipped down over her forehead to anchor her in place during the catapult takeoff. As her seat faced backwards, there would have been no support for her head during the immense acceleration.

Daniel wondered just how much had been done to this particular aircraft to make it aircraft-carrier capable. Trap hook, head straps, structural reinforcements. All he knew was it was the only small business jet that could get them across the northern Pacific Ocean in a single pass without landing for refueling, and that could travel at nearly the speed of sound while doing it.

"Useful," Daniel managed. He'd learned a dozen words in Korean, which thankfully he hadn't needed. He'd actually been banking on his French or German being sufficient as Kim Jong-Un had been educated in Switzerland. Alice had picked up the language for the fun of it, one of the reasons for her transfer to the North Korean desk at the CIA. She did know more about the Supreme Leader than most Americans, maybe more than most people on the planet.

"Do you know anything about basketball?"

Daniel just shook his head. He knew there was a team based in D.C., but that was about all he really knew. He hadn't attended but one or two games in college.

"Major Henderson," Alice leaned across the aisle toward him.

Daniel became dreamily mesmerized by her long, elegant neck and thinking of the way she moaned quietly when he kissed her there. He slid his feet forward and they hugged ankle to ankle.

"Are you a basketball fan?"

"Sure. Don't have much time to catch games, but I follow it."

She aimed one of those radiant Alice smiles at the Major.

Daniel felt drifty as he considered the possible uselessness of being jealous of a happily married man who could probably beat the crap out of him using only one pinky. Daniel tried to imagine their battle, himself in heavy armor with an array of lethal weaponry and Major Mark Henderson, the most decorated pilot in SOAR with his pinky. Daniel made a couple bets with himself on how many seconds it might or might not last. Under ten seconds before Daniel was down and done? Fifty-fifty. Under twenty seconds? No contest at all. He'd be a little smear on this amazingly comfortable seat that was rapidly sucking the willpower out of his bones.

"Did you know," Alice continued in her sweetest voice to Mark, "that Kim Jong-Un became a crazy basketball fan while going to school in Switzerland? And that channel 56 is running the UCLA versus USC game right now?"

Long before any seatbelt sign turned off, Mark had the two guests on the rear sofa and they were all noisily involved in the game on the large-screen TV.

Emily leaned into the aisle toward Alice and whispered, not that the other guys would have heard anything, "That was very well done."

Daniel's sleepy brain wondered if his virility was in question because he didn't troop back to watch the game as well.

Probably.

Chapter 35

Daniel slammed awake and wondered if he really had fought Major Henderson, or even more dangerous, his wife.

Other sensations started penetrating his consciousness.

The engines began winding down.

They weren't moving except for a rock and sway as if a giant rubber band had just grabbed their tail.

There was a strap across his forehead.

The carrier.

He was still in the forward facing seat, which means he'd had to be braced against the sudden deceleration of landing on an aircraft carrier. Someone had strapped his forehead so that the sudden vicious grab of a wire trap wouldn't injure his neck.

He'd slept all of the way across the Pacific, his first decent sleep in several days. Now they were on the U.S.S. John C. Stennis which had just finished unloading most of its jets to the Whidbey Naval Air Station in Washington state's Puget Sound. This was a common practice when coming into port; done in order to avoid flight deck operations inside civilian air space. Of course, their carrier would now sit for a little more than a day with nothing on its deck but a passenger jet. It would cause no interference with flight operations because all of the other planes would be gone.

This had been his idea, based on something Beale had said. One thing he'd contributed to the strategy rather just being baggage.

Alice no longer sat across from him.

He struggled out of the seat belt to see her chatting with one of the most feared leaders on the planet as if they were old friends. A moment longer, his brain now fully awake, he realized they spoke in English.

Kim Jong-Un's voice came out heavy, deeper than when he'd spoken in his native tongue. He made awkward but clear use of a distinctly British accent. And they were chatting about the best restaurants in Grenoble.

If there was any way Daniel could be more gone on this woman, he didn't know what it might be. Alice had not only just charmed the leader of North Korea to relax enough to reveal that he spoke English. She had also just paved the way to make President Matthews have a much more productive meeting.

They filed off the jet into the late evening light, once again wrapped in coats with hoods up. Their entire end of the flight deck was vacant of service personnel. They crossed to the helicopter tied down along the side of the deck. It was the Majors' other Black Hawk.

Normally they flew them in tandem. For this mission, they'd each left behind their copilots and two of their crew chiefs. This was the "A" team, the very best that SOAR had.

They had separated the helicopters by five thousand miles. One chopper was still parked on the U.S.S. *Harry S. Truman* in the Sea of Japan. The other now sat on the U.S.S. *John C. Stennis* a few dozen miles off Cape Hatteras, the northwestern most point of the continental U.S. Also conveniently close to the Canadian islands.

After staggering about for a minute on a deck far more wind-torn than the Truman's deck, Daniel climbed aboard an indistinguishably lethal copy of the chopper he'd ridden into the heart of North Korea. Accommodations were a little more crowded with Alice aboard, but they were far from the half-dozen troops plus field gear that could squeeze into even a heavily weaponized Black Hawk like the Direct Action Penetrator.

An odd silence settled over them as the helicopter performed the mirror of the movement it had made in North Korea, plunging them down to skim the wave tops before roaring landward. Daniel glanced out the window and what little he could see revealed storm-torn waves.

This time he felt both more and less panic; less for himself, more for any potential danger to Alice. A glance revealed that Alice was enjoying the ride immensely and he did his level best to switch off his over-protective instincts.

Kim Jong-Un and his interpreter appeared completely relaxed and at ease with helicopter flight. Any novelty they found aboard a U.S. military helicopter clearly sated in the first flight, they now settled into patient waiting. Daniel had observed that more and more in non-Western countries. Most other world citizens consistently exhibited a patient self-reliance that Americans somehow lacked.

These reflections carried him through the first half of the thirty-minute flight up the storm-torn Strait of San Juan de Fuca and around the southern tip of Vancouver Island. The second half was spent white-knuckling as the chopper dodged between the ten thousand rocks that were the southern end of the Canadian Gulf Islands. The only radar that was going to spot them would be would be some psychotic fisherman out fishing at night among craggy rocks during a nasty northerly storm.

And he'd also be the only person who would find them if the majors screwed up. If they slammed into a cliff face even a psychotic fisherman would be of little use.

With an abrupt jolt the helicopter slammed him down into his seat. He clenched his hand over Alice's and held on tight as they climbed into the night. With a sharp tilt toward the stern, he lost all sense of motion.

They hovered.

Outside the window he could see that the lights were on up at the big stone house. Warm, inviting, stable lights that didn't bob or weave in the dark of the night.

Chapter 36

"Dinner's in an hour." Emily Beale announced as they managed to close the heavy weathered-pine front door against the roaring night.

"I'll help." Alice felt disoriented as she looked about the house and needed something familiar to anchor her in place.

"Make that forty-five," Beale called out then dropped her voice. "Let's go see what we can rustle up."

Daniel, back on his feet after sleeping like a baby throughout the flight, was making sure that their guests were guided toward their rooms. She left him to it.

The fact that he had never doubted her strategic assessment still floored her. That she'd actually been right, shocked her. That he'd slept with his ankles wrapped around hers for the whole flight on the Gulfstream jet had touched her heart and she'd rather not think about that.

Alice moved to follow Emily to the kitchen. She'd toured the house during their initial daytime survey with Captain Smith, but it looked far different at night. During the day, the light and the outdoor world had dominated. A grand vista of the islands and the waves far below. Wide windows invited those inside to notice the surrounding conifers and lawn.

Now, under the warm glow of tastefully recessed lighting, dark tile and lush wood floors invited her to linger in the nearly opulent warmth. The heavy furniture proffered a welcome, an invitation to settle in with a good book and never move again. The walls between the windows wrapped cozily about the room. They were covered with a mix of Native

American art with its shocking red and black and white contrasts, and tall bookcases almost spilling over with a wide variety of novels and histories revealing the owners' eclectic tastes.

The kitchen continued the theme. The cookbooks on a nicely recessed shelf covered a half dozen cuisines. Yet the size and efficient layout of the kitchen revealed that the family cooked here, rather than some servants.

Emily had already pulled out a big tray of steaks.

"You had this place stocked." Alice couldn't believe she hadn't thought of it.

Emily nodded, "I was the First Lady's chef for three weeks after all."

Alice slapped her forehead eliciting Emily's rare laugh, then reached for an apron. Beale's flying had made national news and her cooking shone front and center in the country's gossip pages. It had all been while the Major performed some secret security assignment that Alice had never uncovered. Alice typically felt disjointed around women like Emily Beale. Alice knew how to handle men. Well, men other than Daniel. But women often eluded her.

Emily Beale felt like the sister she'd never had.

"So what am I making?"

"Steaks for entrée. Can you tackle a garlic pasta for a side? I premade cookie dough, so we can hack some off and make a batch of chocolate chip while everything else cooks."

Alice dug out a large pot and set water to heat on the stove. She scrounged around and came up with garlic, sun-dried tomatoes, a small bundle of basil, and some broccoli. They worked together in companionable silence for a while. Emily rubbed a pepper and sage combination into the meat. Alice floreted the broccoli and started to sliver the basil.

"He's quite in love with you."

Alice would have cut off her finger if she'd been using anything more dangerous than a garlic press at the moment. Instead, it merely slipped from her nerveless fingers to clatter down on the counter spreading tiny splatters of garlic across the broad granite surface.

Gripping the counter edge she managed to turn herself enough to face Beale. Emily was leaning comfortably back against the opposite counter and holding out a large glass of red wine. Alice rarely drank. She grabbed the glass and knocked half of it back, leaving her hard pressed to catch her breath.

"What," she tried to ignore the amount of effort entailed to speak the word. "Whatever gave you that idea?"

Emily smiled. That slow, calm, self-assured smile of a woman who has faced down, well, the President and her husband among others.

"It isn't an idea. It's a fact. I'd have to be blind to not see it. Why don't you?"

Alice took another deep swallow of the wine that did nothing to slake a throat long gone dry.

The door to Alice's right opened, but she couldn't turn away from Emily Beale's brilliant blue gaze.

"Go away," Beale said without looking around.

"Uh…" Alice heard Daniel and did her best not to cringe.

"Come, my friend." Major Henderson cut him off with a fake Texas accent thick enough to deep-fry in hot oil. "We'all better be walkin' in places safe for mere men to tread. Which does not include our continued existence if we should remain in this here kitchen."

The door swung closed and silence once again reigned in the kitchen other than the soft sizzle of steaks on iron and the bubbling of the pasta water nearing a boil.

"Just asking." Emily turned back to preparing a bowl of salad with wild greens, hazelnuts, and dried cranberries.

Even as she struggled against the idea of love in her life, Alice's analyst mode kicked in.

Emily Beale, she knew, ranked as an exceptionally acute observer, just one of many areas in which her file stated she ranked far above the norm. She had known Daniel when they were both working for the First Lady. Beale had a frame of reference that spanned the year following as well.

Alice had… What? Her own clear sense that she was not capable of falling in love. And the certainty that no one could ever love her. Not the firmest logic. It was like saying, if A equals B and X is not equal to forty-two, then L must be false. Logic simply didn't work that way.

She tried flipping her thoughts to a more intuitive framework, one that served her well enough to identify Kim Jong-un's desire to speak with the President in private. One that observed Daniel grabbing her hand when panicked in flight, or protecting her during the simulated helicopter attack, of his hand frozen above the first small door of an exquisite Advent Calendar. Three weeks and she still hadn't been able to forget that moment.

Never in her life had she imagined that Dr. Alice Thompson had the ability to freeze a man in his place. Her parents had made it clear that her place in the world would never include a relationship. That love was a façade.

Every one of her friends loved Alice's parents. They were perfect hosts. Intelligent, funny, friendly. Everyone always told her that she was lucky to have such parents. For a father who retreated into impenetrable silence the instant the guest left. Or the harpy with a martini in one hand and a list of Alice's on-going faults in the other.

Not for her. Never that trap.

Once again Emily was facing her. A glass of wine in her own hand.

"I don't like where my thoughts are going."

Emily nodded, "Probably means they are on the right track at last."

"How do I know?" Alice turned the question about. "How did you know?"

Emily's face shifted, a gentle smile revealing a softness difficult to equate with the SOAR major; a smile that shifted her eyes from bright blue to misty summer sky.

"I didn't. I had to beat the shit out of Mark before he convinced me."

If that was a dreamy memory, Alice wasn't sure if she wanted to know the rest of the story. But she couldn't help but be cheered by Emily's obvious good mood.

"So, that's how majors choose a mate?"

"A lifemate. Oh yeah. Absolutely. How about brilliant and beautiful CIA analysts? How do they do it?"

"Carefully." Alice replied even as she fought against the echo of Beale's correction. "A lifemate," she tried the word out. A strange and foreign word. Her parents were married for life, that had become clear years before, but it was more of a life-inmate arrangement, locked in a mutual prison that neither knew how to break.

Emily moved around her to drop the pasta into the rolling water.

Alice finished the garlic, set it beside the diced tomatoes and basil. She grated a couple cups of parmesan cheese. She felt better, more stable. This time she was able to sip her wine. Which was a good thing, as she could definitely feel that initial slug loosening her brain.

"I don't want to be in love with him."

"Why not?" Beale flipped the steaks.

"You're bloody relentless, aren't you?"

"Special Forces pilot. Who knew I'd be like that?"

Emily left Alice with the relentless silence of her own thoughts. Really unfair.

She knew she wasn't in love. She knew she couldn't be.

She also couldn't shake the sneaking suspicion that she was wrong on both counts.

Chapter 37

It was an early night for everyone. Late evening in the Canadian Gulf Islands, late afternoon in North Korea at the end of a long day, and little or no sleep the prior night.

North Korea's leader hadn't been rude at dinner, but he'd made it clear that if it wasn't about basketball, he wouldn't be talking to anyone other than President Matthews.

Daniel offered Alice a separate room. The gentlemanly thing to do, and there were just enough beds. Big John and Tim, the two crew chiefs, had bedded down in bunk beds, generous enough for John's tall frame. Beale and Henderson in one suite, Kim Jong-Un in one of similar comfort and style. Daniel and the Korean bodyguard, who had still remained nameless, were to share another bunk room.

The crew chiefs and the Korean guard had found some degree of trust and set up a schedule so that two could sleep and one patrol.

He gave Alice the last bedroom, which sported a frilly set of curtains and a double bed with pink and pale blue pillows. Clearly a girl's room, the nicest in his estimation. He set out a glass of water and a small collection of fine chocolates as he'd done for the others. Sometimes it was the little touches that counted.

He debated at length about just setting a chocolate and glass for himself on the other side, but it felt presumptuous.

She'd been strangely silent during dinner and it had been left to himself and Henderson to carry the conversation. Tim and John had chipped in with stories of their more famous escapades as the self-declared pranksters of SOAR's fifth battalion. Something about painting a general's Humvee bright pink, every single part right down to the insides of the panels and the under the armor. They'd fully disassembled it to make sure no piece was missed.

"He had a bad habit of calling SOAR pilots 'pansy girls' compared with the 101st airborne." Tim had clearly been deeply insulted.

"Along the way, we may have happened to rebuild the steering system so that the steering wheel worked in reverse. But maybe that wasn't us." John ended wistfully. Tim had cut his steak in a thoughtful silence that spoke volumes.

No one had anything to say, and no one had the energy to fill the lagging gaps in the conversation.

All in all, everyone was relieved when it was bedtime.

Daniel had helped Mark with the dishes. By the time they were done, everyone had retired.

Mark slipped into his and Beale's suite, the lights already out.

Daniel took a quick turn of the house. Lights were out under all the doors, except one.

Alice's door stood open just an inch. A thin beam of light slid out into the hallway.

He peeked in through the crack.

Alice was under the covers, already asleep.

The light that shone through the crack came from the other side of the bed. There, beneath the soft light stood a half-empty glass of water and half of the chocolates he'd left for Alice. The cover was folded back and his travel bag rested on a chair by the window.

He closed the door and slipped into bed beside her as gently as he could.

She mumbled something as he clicked off the light. It took him a moment to unravel that she'd said, "I'm awake."

"Sure you are." He whispered back, gently patting the pleasing round of her hip where it shaped the quilt beside him.

With a soft sigh she settled into a truly deep sleep.

Daniel, perhaps due to sleeping on the jet plane, lay wide awake long into the night.

Chapter 38

Daniel woke briefly and thought he heard the sound of fading helicopter rotors, but the night was dark and the howl of the wind a low moan that whipped sounds out of their normal shape, spattering them across the night sky.

It was light when he awoke alone. This time he did hear rotors. Distinct, the heavy thud of a Black Hawk pounding the air. An arriving helicopter.

He whipped out of bed, checked his watch, and decided he'd be much better off if he caught a shower later. Dressed in two minutes, teeth and hair brushed by three, he met President Matthews and Secret Service agent Frank Adams at the front door.

"Good morning, Daniel."

"Good morning, Mr. President." Daniel could see the majors and their crew chiefs tying down the helicopter under a heavy sky, which was now shedding snow flurries among the morning's icy rain.

The President looked comfortable and easy in the long blue parka more fit for a polar expedition than crossing the front lawn. He'd have slept aboard Air Force One while at McChord Air Force Base. A training ride with his childhood friend Major Emily Beale would not look out of the ordinary when she arrived unexpectedly at the co-located Fort Lewis; unexpectedly and right on schedule.

Frank Adams entered the house before he allowed the President across the threshold. After careful inspection of the entryway and hall closet, he nodded that the President could come this far and no farther. He moved on to inspect the living room

Daniel heard Alice's bright voice answered by the much deeper voice of the Supreme Leader of North Korea as they entered from the kitchen.

Ignoring Frank's protest, the President breezed over to meet his guest.

Daniel offered the agent a sympathetic look.

Before the President led his guest into the study, Frank did manage to check it out. Daniel watched his rapid and intense inspection. A leather and cherry wood theme decorated the office, that had been painted in a surprising pastel that offset the substantial furniture quite nicely. A woman's touch.

Alice's hand rested on his arm as the door closed.

"Are they settled?"

"I suppose."

"Ten people know."

Daniel nodded. Then paused. "Eleven people know. Beale's crew of four, two leaders, two bodyguards, the two of us, and the CIA Director."

Alice tipped her head down, letting those bangs swirl forward, but he stooped to keep a clear view of her face.

"You never told your boss."

She shrugged. "Seemed appropriate."

He kissed her on the forehead. "You done great, Dr. Thompson."

"You too, Dr. Darlington."

They both glanced at the door, where Frank Adams had stationed himself solidly before the threshold. The Secret Service agent, despite being in his forties, was immensely fit and towered like a temple guardian statue. The inner sanctum was not to be disturbed.

Kim Jong-Un's bodyguard was not nearly so vigilant.

A poker game quickly formed in the kitchen. Apparently Seo-yun, having relaxed sufficiently to speak his name, was eager to learn how to fleece his fellow countrymen upon his return. Henderson and the crew chiefs appeared more than happy to oblige him with a few lessons. Daniel just hoped the man had been fortunate enough to bring no money to America. The fact that no bank in the country could exchange North Korean Won notes wouldn't have stopped them from taking every one they could.

In moments a noisy game ensued and was in full swing along with glasses of soda and mugs of hot tea, a large pile of American candy bars close by Seo-yun.

Daniel landed on the living room couch for lack of anything else to do. He had a thousand memos, phone calls, e-mails... all begging for his attention. And with what might be occurring behind the closed study doors, Daniel couldn't think straight long enough to deal with a single one.

When he gave up and shut off his computer he became aware of Alice sitting on the other end of the sofa chatting quietly with Emily Beale. They too were constantly casting sidelong glances at the door.

Daniel went over to fireplace that someone else had lit and fed it a log it didn't really need.

That was how their day went. Reading, chatting, sitting blankly. When Daniel, Emily, and Alice made lunch for everyone, the game broke up. After delivering two trays into the study, someone raided the extensive DVD collection. But no one could really focus.

The tension built inside throughout the day as the storm built outside. The rising howl of the storm sheeted freezing rain against the windows. The waves, only a few hundred feet away and fifty feet below, were rarely visible through the blurred glass. High winds sent the rain across the lawn in mesmerizing waves that held others as rapt as it held Daniel.

Daniel just wanted to curl up on a couch somewhere with Alice. This was why animals hibernated, to avoid storms like this one.

The weather peaked mid-afternoon with a final blast that shook the house and would have cut the power had it been provided by power lines rather than a sturdy diesel generator.

As the day's light faded toward evening, the indistinct murmur of voices from the study stopped. When at last the door opened, everyone had gathered in the living room.

Daniel noticed that the President, despite his usual ability to appear totally unflappable, was sagging beneath his upbeat attitude. Kim Jong-un, still weeks from his thirtieth birthday also appeared exhausted as if the two of them had wrestled desperately with matters of great importance and only together beat them into submission.

The two of them stopped just past the door, Frank Adams now standing close behind, the rest of them forming a loose arc around the living room.

"Well," the President glanced at the Supreme Leader and they traded a silent nod. "There is much work to be done. And perhaps now less to fear. Time is needed. Time and common sense. You have all done a great job."

"Yes." Kim Jong-un clearly didn't want to leave the stage solely to the President. "Progress. Perhaps the beginning of partnership. Much work yet from what you might call friendship. But progress. Yes, fine work. You have good people, Mr. President."

"Thank you, Supreme Leader."

They shook hands once more. Daniel wondered if there could be a more important political moment in recent history, and yet there was not a camera to be seen.

"Now!" the President clapped his hands together. "We need to get off this island. How do we do that?"

Chapter 39

Earlier this morning, Emily's SOAR team had flown the President and Frank Adams back to McChord, just over an hour round trip and no one the wiser. Apparently President Peter Matthews had spent the day aboard Air Force One with a head cold.

With the President gone, Kim Jong-un had collapsed into a deep armchair, making no more pretense of how exhausting the meeting had been. Whatever work they'd done, it had been hard on both men. Good work often was.

The majors had fought their way back through the storm as if it were a quiet summer's day and merely a routine flight.

On their return, Emily had handed Daniel a FedEx package.

Alice saw that it had been addressed to Daniel, in care of Major Beale at McChord. Beale had looked at Daniel strangely as he tucked it under his arm. Alice barely saw that the return address was Tennessee before it was out of sight.

When she'd looked up, she came under the penetrating inspection of Major Emily Beale, and she'd be damned if she knew why. Alice felt like a bug facing a windshield.

Then, a moment later, Alice stood at the door of the island house, waving politely to Supreme Leader Kim Jong-un's back. He merely huddled against the sleet, the umbrella she'd provided to his bodyguard remained useless in the chaotic winds shooting over the sea cliff to swirl wildly between the house and trees.

He had thanked her most politely upon learning she was the analyst who had made this all happen. But now that he was out the door, he clearly just wanted to be out of the weather, into the Black Hawk, and homeward bound.

Which was fine with her.

She closed the front door and leaned back against it with a gasp of relief.

Despite the horrid weather, the crew was departing to head out to the carrier parked off the coast. There they'd board the Gulfstream jet back to the Sea of Japan and deliver the North Koreans home. They'd left in the middle of one night and would be returning in the middle of another two days later.

Daniel had offered to accompany them on the return flight into Korea, but Emily had vetoed it. The weather was bad enough that they didn't want to risk the extra weight of Daniel and Alice aboard the helicopter. That had meant only two passengers to McChord for the return trip to D.C. and only two out to the aircraft carrier where a passenger jet waited on the flight deck for the return trip to Korea.

Finding some reservoir of energy Alice couldn't tap to save her life, Daniel had swept through the house stripping beds, turning off lights, tossing dirty dishes into the dishwasher.

Alone.

They were alone in the house.

She and Daniel.

And would be for at least one day and more likely two until the majors returned from their second flight into the Korean night or the storm broke enough for Captain Nathaniel Smith to fly out from Vancouver and fetch them.

Marooned on a Canadian island with Daniel.

She could think of many things that she did and didn't want to do with Daniel. She wanted to curl up against that beautiful chest and just weep with exhaustion. Ever since she'd seen that first message out of North Korea that had sent her scrambling to the White House, she'd barely slept. And assuming that the Majors flew as safely as they always did, it had all worked.

Another part of her wanted to make love to Daniel until she was too exhausted to either weep or laugh.

And there was the problem.

"Make love to."

She'd never "made love to" anyone. Sex. Sure. Amend that. With Daniel? Mind-bogglingly good sex. Who knew her body could even feel that good?

Alice reached deep and tried to wake her analyst's mind, but wasn't having a lot of luck with that. Instead, she leaned against the closed front door, and did her best not to think.

Finally at a stop, her body took over and noticed the smell that had come slowly wafting out into the living room. Burgers. Food. Her stomach loudly reminded her of its empty state; none of them had done more than nibble at their lunches during the meeting. And everyone else had left before dinner.

She trailed her way into the kitchen. In some ways not so different from the kitchen in the third-floor Residence of the White House. A little more country kitchen than elegant interior decor, but both were small enough to create a cozy, intimate feel.

Daniel had set two plates on the counter. Full service with folded napkins, silverware, water and wine glasses. He'd even scared up a few Christmas decorations now that the North Koreans were gone. A small family of elves and reindeer sat at the far end of the island. Daniel has set them up with tiny plates and their own six-inch tall Christmas tree.

For the humans at the table, he'd made a delicate salad in wooden bowls. And on the plate rested toasted burger buns and a pile of golden-brown French fries.

"Will you—" Alice clamped her teeth down on her tongue in a hurry. She'd almost jokingly asked if he'd marry her. It would be funny in any other situation when a man cooked something that smelled this good. She would have said it if Emily Beale hadn't stood right where Daniel now flipped burgers and asked Alice what she was going to do about Daniel being in love with her.

What was she going to do?

She didn't want her mother's past. Or her father's. Trapped in a life neither of them understood. They'd started out happy. She'd seen the photos. The video of the wedding. Listened to them laugh, actually laugh together, as they filmed their only daughter's first steps. A joy between them that had long since passed into the realm of impossible. So far gone that it was now unimaginable despite the evidence caught on tape.

Whatever they'd had was long dead.

Alice had sworn she'd never make that mistake.

But would she?

Was she capable of making that mistake, of letting love die?

Would Daniel even let her screw it up that badly? This was a man who loved family. A grown man who had his family's and his big sister's photos on his dresser. He'd probably find some way to make her happier with each passing year. It poured out of him, straight from his heart. The question was, could she do the same for him?

Hadn't she answered her own question last night when she'd left the light on and the door open? His mere presence had unnerved her since Beale's question, but Alice was a better person, far better and far happier with Daniel beside her than when they were apart. And Daniel had chosen to accept the invitation and sleep beside her. She wished she'd had hours to just lie there and watch him sleep.

Daniel served up the burgers, drowned them in sautéed mushrooms, and sat down across the chopping block island from her. He lit two candles and turned off the lights.

Damn, he was turning even a simple dinner into an occasion. A very romantic occasion. Marooned together on a wild but homey island. He looked exhausted, and absolutely, positively stunning. Not just the handsome man who sat across from her. She also saw the man who both helped a President rule and made her feel as if she had a home she'd never imagined. And he made both look effortless.

Comfort food. Daniel had made them comfort food.

"What's for dessert?"

He tapped the Advent calendar that was sitting on the corner of the island counter.

"We missed last night, too."

"Gimme!"

Daniel laughed that rolling chuckle of his that made her think of hillsides in the sun.

"Don't you want to eat first?"

"Gimme now!" she pushed aside her plate, folded her arms across her chest, and did her best to pout.

Daniel considered her for a long moment. That smile hiding something. Shifting for just a moment into the White House Chief of Staff mode, despite wearing a turtleneck shirt rather than a suit and tie. But then he shifted back to merely being amused. As if he'd had to adjust some thinking, tweak some master plan. She had to remember that for every molecule of her being that was a supreme analyst, he was a master strategist.

"Here's last night's." He opened a little door at the base of the pictured tree, down among the unwrapped presents. And extracted a pair of dark chocolates. So dark that they looked black under the candlelight.

She didn't raise her hands, but rather leaned forward and took one directly with her teeth, leaving a small nibble on his fingertips in her wake. The chocolate flowed warm, lush, creamy, rich. "That may be the best chocolate I've ever had." She felt as if her body melted into a gentler version of herself along with the chocolate.

He nodded, looking a little dazed himself.

"You," his voice caught. "You can open the last window."

She pulled over the Advent calendar.

Once again she looked at the magnificent final image.

"It's us," Daniel had texted when he saw it. The two young kittens were peeking out from the wrapping paper under the tree, deep in a game of hide-and-pounce. Crinkly balls, feather toys, catnip mice, and more spread far and wide from the tree and across the living room floor.

On a deep, embroidered pillow, before the crackling fire, the mama and papa cat curled together. It was impossible to tell quite where one began and the other ended. Painted so finely that she wanted to stroke their fur.

That Daniel saw the two of them that way had actually made her heart hurt. She had to cover it again with her hand to keep it in place.

She checked the number on the door that had hidden the dark chocolate. Twenty-three. The next one opened into the side of the pillow on which the two cats curled together.

"The last one. Twenty-four," her voice such a soft whisper even she could barely hear it.

"Christmas eve," Daniel answered little louder.

Alice looked up at Daniel. But his eyes were hidden in candlelit shadows. She wished she could see what was going on in those deep blue eyes of his, but his thoughts remained hidden.

It was always her most important holiday of the year. She'd always loved Christmas, even though she'd usually celebrated alone. But the last weeks had become so frantic that she'd lost all track of time. She hadn't even finished the snowflake mittens she'd been knitting as a surprise for Daniel.

She'd barely started her special project. She'd missed her favorite season of the year. A small price, she supposed, for making the world a safer place.

"Tomorrow we'll be spending Christmas together." Alice realized. "Just us." There was a bright side. She could think of no one else she'd rather spend it with.

He nodded toward the calendar with a "go ahead" gesture.

Taking a deep breath, she pulled open the last door.

"It was my grandmother's. I had my sister send it. I texted her right before we went into North Korea."

The FedEx package from Tennessee. From Daniel's home.

She pulled the circle of gold from the recess. A trio of small diamonds in a simple band. Not posh. Not gaudy. Absolutely elegant. Absolutely Daniel.

Alice looked at it sparkle in the candlelight.

Daniel was anchored in the past. Family. Tradition. Honor. Love.

Her past... Well, she wouldn't be anchored by it. Not any longer. She would cut that cable.

"Here," she handed the ring to Daniel.

He took it tentatively. His brief look of worry cleared as she held out her left hand.

She had cut the cable and was now flying free.

Daniel slid the warm gold over her ring finger and anchored it in place with a kiss.

Alice and Daniel.

They'd soar straight up into the night sky.

"Tomorrow," she told the man still holding her hand so tightly, "we'll be spending our first of many Christmases together."

END NOTE

Yes, the stone house exists. Years ago I sailed around this steep island deep in the heart of the Canadian Gulf Islands. It did indeed have towering cliffs, a dock crane, helipad, and sweeping lawn leading up to a beautiful house, surrounded on three sides by Douglas fir trees towering eighty feet or more above. I have never visited there, but I'd love to someday. Looking fantastically romantic, it always struck me as the perfect place to celebrate a cozy Christmas. It just took me twenty years for this image to find the right story.

ABOUT THE AUTHOR

M. L. Buchman has worked in fast food, law, opera, computers, publishing, and light manufacturing. It's amazing what you can do with a degree in geophysics. Burnt out on the corporate ladder, he sold everything and spent 18 months riding a bicycle around the world. In 11,000 miles, he touched 15 countries and hundreds of amazing people. Since then, he has acquired a loving lady, the coolest kid on the planet, and lives in Portland, Oregon.

More at: www.mlbuchman.com

EXCERPT FROM:
WHERE DREAMS ARE BORN
by M.L. Buchman

Russell locked his door behind the last of the staff and turned off his camera. He knew it was good. The images were there. He'd really captured them.

But something was missing.

The groove ran so clean when he slid into it. The studio faded into the background, then the strobe lights, reflector umbrellas, and blue and green backdrops all became texture and tone.

Image, camera, man became one and they were all that mattered; a single flow of light beginning before time was counted and ending in the printed image. A ray of primordial light traveling forever to glisten off the BMW roadster still parked in one corner of the wood-planked studio. Another ray lost in the dark blackness of the finest leather bucket seats. One more picking out the supermodel's perfect hand dangling a single, shining, golden key. The image shot just slow enough that they key blurred as it spun, but the logo remained clear.

He couldn't quite put his finger on it...

Another great ad by Russell Morgan. Russell Morgan, Inc. The client would be knocked dead, and the ad leaving all others standing still as it roared down the passing lane. Might get him another Clio, or even a second Mobius.

But... There wasn't usually a "but."

The groove had definitely been there, but he hadn't been in it. That was the problem. It had slid along, sweeping his staff into their own orchestrated perfection, but he'd remained untouched. Not part of that ideal, seamless flow.

"Be honest, boyo, that session sucked," he told the empty studio. Everything had come together so perfectly for yet another ad for yet another high-end glossy. Man, the Magazine would launch spectacularly in a few weeks, a high-profile mid-December launch, a never before seen twelve page spread by Russell Morgan, Inc. and the rag would probably never pay off the lavish launch party of hope, ice sculptures, and chilled magnums of champagne before disappearing like a thousand before it.

He stowed the last camera he'd been using with the others piled by his computer. At the breaker box he shut off the umbrellas, spots, scoops, and washes. The studio shifted from a stark landscape in hard-edged relief to a nest of curious shadows and rounded forms. The tang of hot metal and deodorant were the only lasting result of the day's efforts.

"Morose tonight, aren't we?" he asked his reflection in the darkened window of his Manhattan studio. His reflection was wise enough to not answer back. There wasn't ever a "down" after a shoot, there had always been an "up."

Not tonight. He'd kept everyone late, even though it was Thanksgiving eve, hoping for that smooth slide of image, camera, man. It was only when he saw the power of the images he captured that he knew he wasn't a part of the chain anymore and decided he'd paid enough triple-time expenses.

The single perfect leg wrapped in thigh-high red-leather boots visible in the driver's seat. The sensual juxtaposition of woman and sleek machine. An ad designed to wrap every person with even a hint of a Y-chromosome around its little finger. And those with only X-chromosomes would simply want to be her. A perfect combo of sex for the guys and power for the women.

Russell had become no more than the observer, the technician behind the camera. Now that he faced it, months, maybe even a year had passed since he'd been yanked all the way into the light-image-camera-man slipstream. Tonight was the first time he hadn't even trailed in the churned up wake.

"You're just a creative cog in the advertising photography machine." Ouch! That one stung, but it didn't turn aside the relentless steamroller of his thoughts speeding down some empty, godforsaken autobahn.

0okgo now

His career was roaring ahead, his business fast and smooth, but, now that he considered it, he really didn't give a damn.

His life looked perfect, but—"Don't think it!" —but his autobahn mind finished, "it wasn't."

Russell left his silent reflection to its own thoughts and went through the back door that led to his apartment, closing it tightly on the perfect BMW, the perfect rose on the seat, and somewhere, lost among a hundred other props from dozens of other shoots, the long pair of perfect red-leather Chanel boots that had been wrapped around the most expensive legs in Manhattan. He didn't care if he never walked back through that door again. He'd been doing his art by rote, how God-awful sad was that?

And he shot commercial art. He'd never had the patience to do art for art's sake. No draw for him. No fire. He left the apartment dark, only a soft glow from the blind-covered windows revealing the vaguest outlines of the framed art on the wall. Even that almost overwhelmed him.

He didn't want to see the huge prints by the art artists: autographed Goldsworthy, Liebowitz, and Joseph Francis' photomosaics for the moderns. A hundred and fifty more rare, even one of a kind prints, all the way back through Bourke-White to his prize, an original Daguerre. The collection that the Museum of Modern Art kept begging him to let them borrow for a show. He bypassed the circle of chairs and sofas that could be a playpen for two or a party for twenty. He cracked the fridge in the stainless steel and black kitchen searching for something other than his usual beer.

A bottle of Krug.

Maybe he was just being grouchy after a long day's work.

Milk.

No. He'd run his enthusiasm into the ground but good.

Juice even.

Would he miss the camera if he never picked it up again?

No reaction.

Nothing.

Not even a twinge.

That was an emptiness he did not want to face. Alone, in his apartment, in the middle of the world's most vibrant city.

Russell turned away, and just as the door swung closed, the last sliver of light, the relentless cold blue-white of the refrigerator bulb, shone across his bed. A quick grab snagged the edge of the door and left the narrow beam illuminating a long pale form on his black bedspread.

The Chanel boots weren't in the studio. They were still wrapped around those three thousand dollar-an-hour legs. The only clothing on a perfect body, five foot-eleven of intensely toned female anatomy, right down to her exquisitely stair-mastered behind. Her long, white-blond hair, a perfect Godiva over the tanned breasts. Except for their too exact symmetry, even the closest inspection didn't reveal the work done there. One leg raised just ever so slightly to hide what was meant to be revealed later. Discovered.

Melanie.

By the steady rise and fall of her flat stomach, he knew she'd fallen asleep, waiting for him to finish in the studio.

How long had they been an item? Two months? Three?

She'd made him feel alive. At least when he was with her. The super-model in his bed. On his arm at yet another SoHo gallery opening, dazzling New York's finest at another three-star restaurant, wooing another gathering of upscale people with her ever so soft, so sensual, so studied French accent. Together they were wired into the heart of the in-crowd.

But that wasn't him, was it? It didn't sound like the Russell he'd once known.

Perhaps "they" were about how he looked on her arm?

Did she know tomorrow was the annual Thanksgiving ordeal at his parents? That he'd rather die than attend? Any number of eligible woman floating about who'd finagled an invitation in hopes of snaring one of People Magazine's "100 Most Eligible." Heir to a billion or some such, but wealthy enough on his own, by his own sweat. Number twenty-four this year, up from forty-seven the year before despite Tom Cruise being available yet again.

No.

Not Melanie. It wasn't the money that drew her. She wanted him. But more she wanted the life that came with him, wrapped in the man package. She wanted The Life. The one that People Magazine readers dreamed about between glossy pages.

His fingertips were growing cold where they held the refrigerator door cracked open.

If he woke her there'd be amazing sex. Or a great party to go to. Or…

Did he want "Or"? Did he want more from her?

Sex. Companionship. An energy, a vivacity, a thirst he feared that he lacked. Yes.

But where hid that smooth synchronicity like light-image-camera-man? Where lurked that perfect flow from one person to another? Did she feel it? Could he... ever again?

"More?" he whispered into the darkness to test the sound.

The door slid shut, escaped from numb fingers, plunging the apartment back into darkness, taking Melanie along with it.

His breath echoed in the vast darkness. Proof that he was alive, if nothing more.

Time to close the studio. Time to be done with Russell Incorporated.

Then what?

Maybe Angelo would know what to do. He always claimed he did. Maybe this time Russell would actually listen to his almost-brother, though he knew from the experience of being himself for the last thirty years that was unlikely. Seattle. Damn! He'd have to go to bloody Seattle to find his best friend.

He could guarantee that wouldn't be a big hit with Melanie.

Now if he only knew if that was a good thing or bad.

# # #

"If you were still alive, you'd pay for this one, Daddy." The moment the words escaped her lips, Cassidy Knowles slapped a hand over her mouth to negate them, but it was too late.

The sharp wind took her words and threw them back into the trees, guilt and all. It might have stopped her, if it didn't make this the hundredth time she'd cursed him this morning.

She leaned in and forged her way downhill until the muddy path broke free from the mossy smell of the trees. Her Stuart Weitzman boots were long since soaked through, and now her feet were freezing. The two-inch heels had nearly flipped her into the mud a dozen different times.

Cassidy Knowles stared at the lighthouse. It perched upon a point of rock, tall and white, with its red roof as straight and snug as a prim bonnet. A narrow trail traced along the top of the breakwater leading to the lighthouse. The parking lot, much to her chagrin, was empty; six, beautiful, empty spaces.

"Sorry, ma'am," park rangers were always polite when telling you what you couldn't do. "The parking lot by the light is for physically-challenged visitors only. You'll have to park here. It is just a short walk to the lighthouse."

The fact that she was dressed for a nice afternoon lunch at Pike Place Market safe in Seattle's downtown rather than a blustery mile-long walk on the first day of the year didn't phase the ranger in the slightest.

Cassidy should have gone home, would have if it hadn't been for the letter stuffed deep in her pocket. So, instead of a tasty treat in a cozy deli, she'd buttoned the top button of her suede Bernardo jacket and headed down the trail. At least the promised rain had yet to arrive, so the jacket was only cold, not wet. The stylish cut had never been intended to fight off the bajillion mile-an-hour gusts that snapped it painfully against her legs. And her black leggings ranged about five layers short of tolerable and a far, far cry from warm.

At the lighthouse, any part of her that had been merely numb slipped right over to quick frozen. Leaning into the wind to stay upright, tears streaming from her eyes, she could think of a thing or two to tell her father despite his recent demise and her general feelings about the usefulness of upbraiding a dead man.

"What a stupid present!" her shout was torn word-by-word, syllable-by-syllable and sent flying back toward her nice warm car and the smug park ranger.

A calendar. He'd given her a stupid calendar of stupid lighthouses and a stupid letter to open at each stupid one. He'd been very insistent, made her promise. One she couldn't ignore. A deathbed promise.

Other Fine Books by This Author

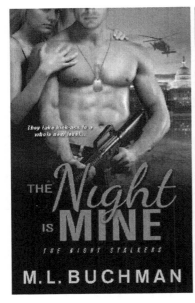

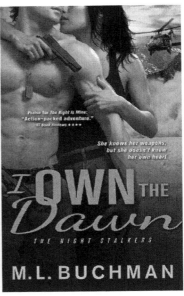

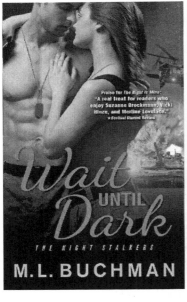

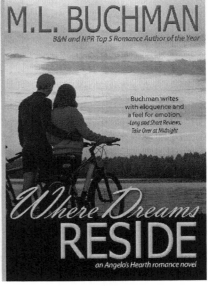

8629

Made in the USA
Lexington, KY
11 February 2016